Torn between two worlds . . .

WATCHING MY WIFE chase after a human boy was hell. The heavy rain drenched the thin fabric of her clothes in seconds, plastering them to her body in a way that would be appealing . . . if *he* wasn't going to see her, too. I clenched my jaw. *She just doesn't want him to get hurt.* It wasn't as though I wanted any mortals caught in the crossfire when we faced Zeus either. Persephone was just going to charm the boy into leaving the park.

Tearing my gaze away from her as she scurried up the hill, I searched the parking lot for Aphrodite, or Zeus, or whoever he, she, it may be. I had the layout of Memorial Park memorized anyway. Who was I kidding? The entire city of Athens, Georgia was embedded in my mind. The precaution was reasonable. Persephone spent most of her time here, and she was a magnet for trouble.

I followed her up the dirt-packed path in my mind's eye. She'd be rounding the corner now well above the park, oblivious to the way the plants she passed leaned toward her. Persephone was beautiful. Vibrant. Light and vitality pulsed from her like the first warm gust of a spring breeze promised everything would soon be new and alive again, that winter would thaw into life. Everything was drawn to her. Unfortunately.

———

"If you love Greek mythology and young adult books, this series is a perfect choice!"
—Jess at *Such A Novel Idea*

"What a powerful whirlwind end to this section of the series! . . . There's so much heartbreak in this book. So much emotion. A great book!"
—*Reader's Dialogue*

The Daughters of Zeus Series
by Kaitlin Bevis

Persephone

Daughter of Earth and Sky

The Iron Queen

The Iron Queen

The Daughters of Zeus Series
Book Three

by

Kaitlin Bevis

ImaJinn Books

This is a work of fiction. Names, characters, places and incidents are either the products of the author's imagination or are used fictitiously. Any resemblance to actual persons (living or dead), events or locations is entirely coincidental.

IMAJINN

ImaJinn Books
PO BOX 300921
Memphis, TN 38130
Print ISBN: 978-1-61194-801-1

ImaJinn Books is an Imprint of BelleBooks, Inc.

The Daughters of Zeus trilogy was originally published in ebook-only by Musa Press.

ImaJinn Books was founded by Linda Kichline.

We at ImaJinn Books enjoy hearing from readers. Visit our websites
ImaJinnBooks.com
BelleBooks.com
BellBridgeBooks.com

10 9 8 7 6 5 4 3 2 1

Cover design: Debra Dixon
Interior design: Hank Smith
Photo/Art credits:
Woman (manipulated) © Inara Prusakova | Dreamstime.com
Woman (manipulated) © Syda Productions | Dreamstime.com
Texture (manipulated) © Olgakorneeva | Dreamstime.com
Frame © Liudmila Metaeva | Renderosity

:Lqij:01:

Dedication

To Mrs. Saul's fourth block freshmen. You guys were amazing. Thank you for putting up with me for an entire semester.

And to my readers. You have no idea how much I value your reviews and insights.

vi

Chapter I

Hades

WATCHING MY WIFE chase after a human boy was hell. The heavy rain drenched the thin fabric of her clothes in seconds, plastering them to her body in a way that would be appealing . . . if *he* wasn't going to see her, too. I clenched my jaw. *She just doesn't want him to get hurt.* It wasn't as though I wanted any mortals caught in the crossfire when we faced Zeus either. Persephone was just going to charm the boy into leaving the park.

Tearing my gaze away from her as she scurried up the hill, I searched the parking lot for Aphrodite, or Zeus, or whoever he, she, it may be. I had the layout of Memorial Park memorized anyway. Who was I kidding? The entire city of Athens, Georgia was embedded in my mind. The precaution was reasonable. Persephone spent most of her time here, and she was a magnet for trouble.

I followed her up the dirt-packed path in my mind's eye. She'd be rounding the corner now well above the park, oblivious to the way the plants she passed leaned toward her. Persephone was beautiful. Vibrant. Light and vitality pulsed from her like the first warm gust of a spring breeze that promised everything would soon be new and alive again, that winter would thaw into life. Everything was drawn to her. Unfortunately.

My thoughts returned to the human boy she was following. I scowled. Rain fell, pinging against the transparent shield that kept me out of sight while I sat dry atop a metal picnic table. My fingers worried at a spot of rust. I tried not to think too hard about whatever else might have touched the shining surface.

This realm was disgusting. Insects swarmed the park, and birds flew through the air, dropping waste indiscriminately onto the world below. I couldn't wait to return to the Underworld. The surface had its charms, but I had no desire to stay for long.

Joel!

Persephone's voice rang through my mind, and I tossed up a mental wall. It wasn't just good manners preventing me from listening in. This boy had been in her thoughts every night. I'd seen the way he looked at her like she was something to be consumed, the way he touched her like her body was his for the taking, the way her heart raced when she felt his breath upon her neck. I clenched my jaw and studied the parking lot like it might change shape any moment.

She'd probably think less of me if I ripped him apart.

Not that her opinion was all that stopped me. It wasn't my habit to go around killing mortal children, and not just because I'd have to deal with them in the Underworld. I liked humans. Just not when they groped my wife.

My heart thudded at an uncomfortable speed, filling my body with adrenaline. I couldn't seem to catch my breath. My hands gripped the edge of the picnic table, and I leaned forward, muscles tensed. That was strange. I had no reason to be this anxious. He was just a kid, and Persephone was Persephone, she had no idea what affect she had. I couldn't really fault him for being interested, and I had encouraged her to see other people. A spectacularly stupid move on my part. Not only was it condescending as hell to tell Persephone what she should and shouldn't feel toward me, but I'd managed to push her into the arms of another man. It had taken all of two seconds for me to realize I *really* didn't want her to be with other men.

Apparently on top of all my other charming flaws I'm over-possessive. Who knew?

I took a deep breath to force myself to calm down, but it didn't seem to work. What was the matter with me? Channeling Persephone's power away every night had given me a very unwanted front row seat to her developing relationship with Joel. I'd seen every kiss, everything, and not felt *this* before. It hadn't been pleasant, but—

Cold dread filled the pit of my stomach, and I frowned. This didn't even feel like rage. My heart was still beating a mile a minute, like it might burst free from my chest at the slightest provocation. I felt strange, no . . . *terrified*.

That was it. Fear. But why was I—?

It wasn't mine.

My thoughts flew to Persephone, crashing through the mental wall. Her abject terror flooded my thoughts with such paralyzing force that for a second I lost the ability to move or breathe. All that existed was her fear. The boy spoke in a harsh voice, grip tight on her arm. I rose from the picnic table, ready to relieve him of that limb, when his words filtered through her thoughts.

. . . Hades.

I blinked. *How would he know my name?*

A red sports car squealed into the parking lot, and I swore. *Hate to interrupt,* I directed the thought to Persephone.

The boy locked gazes with Persephone and seemed to look through her to me. I knew those eyes. Images and thought fragments flashed from Persephone's mind to catch me up, but I already knew everything I needed to.

Persephone, run! I tore through the parking lot to reach the path.

Hades, it's Joel! He's Zeus!

The whole story passed through my mind accompanied by waves of fear and guilt. Persephone gripping Joel's arm to teleport but nothing happening, followed by her realization that Joel wasn't from this realm. Her shock and horror when his glamour melted away. Why wasn't she running?

Get out of there, now!

I couldn't keep the panic out of my thoughts. If Zeus hurt her . . .

Our plan, she protested.

She wouldn't. Only a fool would risk going through with our plan now. We'd intended to trap Zeus by having him stand on an entrance to the Underworld so we could bring some of my realm up and around him. A little slice of Tartarus. It had worked to imprison some of the Titans before, and it could work with him. But not like this. Not with her alone and hopelessly overpowered.

But this was Persephone. The girl who had fled the safety of the Underworld to confront Boreas with nothing but righteous indignation on her side. It was foolish of me to expect her to do anything else.

I swore and scrambled up the hill. *Just teleport. Leave!*

I can get him to the entrance. Hades, this is our best chance.

Her determination pounded through me coupled with her desperate need for this to be over. She wouldn't run. If I couldn't reach her in time . . .

A bright light seared my vision as I rounded the corner. She screamed, intense pain flashing through her and reverberating to me. I stumbled, blinded by her white-hot agony. Another flash. Pain flared through her, exploding within my mind in a cacophony of anguish. My vision cleared for a split second, and I saw the ground rush toward me. Then everything went black.

Chapter II

Aphrodite

PERSEPHONE'S anguished scream echoed through the park. I'd rushed over as soon as she called me for help, but knew I was too late. The air hummed with energy, setting my hair on end as I jumped out of the cherry red convertible I'd "borrowed" from some random guy.

I sloshed onto the wet pavement, twisting my ankle in my haste, and made a mental note not to wear heels next time Persephone needed me.

Not that she made a habit of calling *me* when she needed something. *She must really be desperate.* I hurried up the wooded running path and almost tripped over a crumbled shape. Hades. What could have knocked Hades out?

"Aphrodite." A voice as smooth as silk sent shivers up my spine.

I cast a shield and jumped in front of Hades. Zeus emerged from a grove of trees holding Persephone like some knight out of a painting. Her limp, dangling arms swayed as he walked. Golden hair, so bright against her corpse-pale skin that it didn't look real, cascaded in waves toward the ground. He strode toward me, strong and radiant. Like the sun had reached through him just to get a little closer to earth. The scene would have been breathtaking, like something out of a storybook, if it wasn't for the sinister expression on his face.

Damn it, I'd hoped it would never come to this. She was my sister and my friend, and I'd stabbed her in the back by pretending "Joel" was anyone other than Zeus. Yes, he'd forced me to help him, but that was no excuse. I never wanted Zeus to win. But now he had Persephone, and with her, access to the Underworld *and* the living realm. We were all doomed.

"You said you wouldn't hurt her." I'd meant to sound defiant, angry, but it came out petulant and scared.

"I said I didn't have to. There's a difference."

I closed my eyes. Of course there was. "You're leaving me here, aren't you?"

Zeus grinned. "I'm sure you'll make yourself useful."

I was surprised it still hurt. I'd known from the beginning I was no more than a pawn to Zeus. He'd created me from the remains of Uranus to give me unprecedented levels of charisma and then abandoned me in the world without the knowledge to control the charm.

Charisma, or charm, is kind of like mind control if you know how to use it. I can smile at pretty much any human and make him do what I want, but uncontrolled it's dangerous. Like, Trojan War dangerous. Used without direction, it steers humans toward their baser instincts. They become obsessed. Anything could have happened to me, but either way, it served Zeus' purposes. He had backup plans for his backup plans.

Now he was leaving me with two very pissed off deities who would move heaven and earth to find Persephone. No telling what they'd do to me.

Did Persephone even know how lucky she was? I'd sell my soul for just one of the followers she collected everywhere she went. To be someone worthy of worship instead of the obedient abomination Zeus created, stripped of my free will and forced into servitude.

Zeus shifted and grabbed the necklace Persephone wore. "Tell Hades"—he cast a knowing glance at the shield behind me with a smirk—"and Demeter I'll take their realms in exchange for the girl." The silver chain snapped, and he tossed the necklace toward me. "Give him that."

Before I could answer, he vanished.

Plucking the necklace out of a puddle, I shook water off the small green plant that sat anchored in a wire basket and dried the pomegranate charm on my shirt. Oh yeah. Hades was definitely going to kill me when he came to.

I'd run, but it wasn't like I had a choice. Zeus created me with an extra special tweak. I was loyal to family. Loyal to the point of obedience if they outranked me enough. That was why I was almost glad I was still "useful" to him; I had a feeling the minute he didn't need me anymore, he'd ask me to swear fealty and give him all my power. Suicide by devotion. And I'd have no choice but to oblige.

If I swore over everything to him, would he release my soul to the Underworld? Would I finally be free? Or would he keep me, my thoughts and memories, and everything about me that *was* me locked in his head in case he ever found it useful?

I sat beside Hades and pulled my knees to my chest. Hollow. I felt hollow inside, like Zeus had carved out everything that mattered, every-thing I cared about, and left me empty. Hopeless. The rain dripped down my face, mimicking the tears I didn't dare cry.

Chapter III

Persephone

GETTING STRUCK BY lightning hurts. A lot. Most people die long before they fully process the pain of a storm's worth of voltage passing through their body in the blink of an eye. I don't have that luxury. Instead, I discovered something that hurt far worse than becoming a sadistic deity's living electrical conduit. Healing from a lightning strike at godspeed.

When I came to, my body felt like it was pulsing molten lava through my veins with each heartbeat. *Gods!* An inhuman moan tore from my throat. *What happened?* It wasn't until the bed shifted I realized I wasn't alone.

Hades. I let myself relax. Relief calmed me enough for unconsciousness to threaten to pull me back under, so I forced myself to take steady breaths. It was too soon to open my eyes. I knew how to stay conscious through horrific pain. Thanatos taught me that.

I breathed in too deeply, and a bolt of pain lanced through me. When I shifted positions to get comfortable, a low moan worked its way up my throat. There was no comfortable. The lightning had seared every single nerve ending in my body. Healing from this didn't feel good at all.

His hand brushed the hair out of my face.

"Hades?" I croaked, struggling to open my eyes.

He shushed me, stroking my arm. I leaned into his touch as the memories rushed back—Hades finding out about Thanatos and killing him, destroying his soul, planning to trap Zeus, waiting at the park for Aphrodite, and realizing Joel was there. What happened to Joel?

The voice shushed me again, and the hand on my shoulder didn't feel comforting anymore. His touch felt . . . wrong. My eyes flew open, and I bolted upright.

With a horrible certainty I turned to see who sat next to me on the bed.

Chapter IV

Hades

THE WORDS SWIRLED on the page of the book I read into an indecipherable vortex of black ink. It was obvious I was dreaming, and not just because the brain is incapable of processing the written language in its sleep. I dislike dreaming. With a frustrated sigh, I set down the book, careful not to wake Persephone sleeping beside me even though I knew she wasn't actually here.

My whole body hurt enough that the novelty of feeling physical pain was lost on me. The pain and the dream meant something important, something bad. A deep sleep like this meant I'd lost consciousness somehow. What could hurt *me?*

Beside me, Persephone sighed and moved closer. Yeah, something was wrong. However ambivalent I tried to be in the waking world, the scenarios that played out in my head when I pictured us in bed never featured Persephone sleeping or me reading. In dreams at least, I deserved more action.

I studied her sleeping form, struck by how still she was. Awake, Persephone was in constant motion, so full of life she almost glowed. Beautiful, but sometimes that never ending motion made it hard to just *look* at her. Brushing a strand of hair from her face, I wished I could feel happy, at peace, or what not. Shouldn't I? We were together after all, with all our secrets and hang-ups out in the open at last. Instead, all I felt was dread and fear and pain.

Something was horribly wrong.

She opened her brilliant green eyes and smiled. "Hades."

A shiver went through me at the sound of my name passing through her lips. She sat up, the thin sleeve of her blue nightgown slipping down her left shoulder as she moved. I pushed it up her arm, fingers trailing over her smooth skin.

Her breath caught, a pained sound. I frowned. A deep purple bruise spread from beneath my fingertips, staining her sun-kissed skin.

"How could you?" she whispered.

I glanced up to her in confusion and drew in a sharp breath. My gaze darted from her face, puffy and crisscrossed with lacerations, to her nightgown, torn and bloodied, to her arm hanging limp at her side, the bones poking through the skin at odd angles. "Persephone! What—"

"You didn't stop him." She cried out in pain and hunched forward. I caught her, cradling her bruised and battered body in my arms while blood soaked into the mattress. When I tried to heal her, nothing happened.

Powerless. She was dying in my arms and for the first time in my entire *existence* I was powerless against death. My chest felt tight against my racing heart. "Persephone?" Clutching her to me, I jerked my gaze around the room in an irrational quest to find something, anything that could help her. I *knew* I was dreaming, but it didn't matter. Nothing mattered except the limp, bleeding girl in my arms.

Her bright green eyes were fixed on me in accusation. They flickered then dimmed as her last words echoed around the room.

"How could you?"

Chapter V

Aphrodite

HADES GROANED and shifted positions. I shook his shoulder.

"Hades?"

His eyes snapped open. He bolted up and glanced around the park, gaze falling on a nearby patch of scorched earth. A myriad of emotions flickered over his face, too fast for me to identify. Looking at me, his gaze hardened in rage. "Where is she?"

My voice shook as I held out the necklace. "Zeus will take the Underworld in exchange for—"

I found myself on the ground, Hades' hands wrapped around my throat. Agony spread from his fingertips as they dug into the sensitive skin around my neck, crushing my windpipe. Power pulsed from his hands, setting my entire body ablaze with pain. Beneath me the ground crackled and shriveled. Leaves turned dark with decay.

I screamed, or tried to, but all that came out was a strangled yelp.

"Let's try that again. Where. Is. She?" His voice was dark and dangerous, and there was murder in his eyes.

"With Zeus," I squeaked. I couldn't breathe. I pried at his hands, scratching against his iron fingers so hard my nails bent and broke. Hades didn't budge.

"Where?"

"I don't know." *Oh gods*, it hurt.

"But you can contact him?" He loosened his grip on my neck a fraction.

"Can't—" Coughing, I cleared my throat. My neck burned, and my voice sounded hoarse and scratchy. Pushing away from him to make space to breathe only farther entrenched my body in the damp dirt. Wet leaves clung to my legs, unbothered by my pathetic attempts to kick free. *Oh, what's the point?* I went still beneath him when I realized there was no reason to struggle against someone *so* much stronger than me. As a goddess, I wasn't weak. But that didn't make me a match for Hades.

"Sorry, I can't help you find her."

"You're *sorry?*" His jaw clenched so hard, I was surprised I didn't hear his teeth shatter against the pressure. "When did he come to you? How long have you known Joel was Zeus, and *why* didn't you warn her?"

I shuddered at the memory of the day I met Joel. I'd thought he was human. Then he'd smiled at me, eyes flashing an unearthly blue I'd only ever seen once before—when I was created then abandoned to Poseidon's realm. That was the day I'd learned I had to obey Zeus no matter what. The cruelty in those eyes forged my worst nightmares.

"I didn't know—"

"Didn't know *what?* That he would take her or hurt her, or that he was pretending to be Joel? *What* didn't you know?" Hades drew back, electric blue eyes so full of rage I was blinded to everything else. In that moment, there was no difference between him and Zeus because their eyes were the same. "We warned you Zeus was dangerous. She fought to take you in after everyone else told her not to trust you. And after *everything* Persephone did for you, you pushed her toward him! Why?"

"He's our father!" My voice broke.

"You honestly think he gives a damn about you?" Hades hauled me to my feet and shoved me down the path of damp packed earth where weak sunlight filtered through the trees, barely breaking through the clouds. "Fine, then let's trade you for her. How loud do you think you'll have to scream to get his attention?" Black energy sparked from his fingertips, dancing up his palm like lightning set on fire.

I stumbled away from Hades, holding my hands out as if that would keep him at bay. "I'm not stupid!" I snapped. "If he cared about me at all, he wouldn't leave me here with *you.*"

Fury contorted Hades' features. His dark hair stuck to his face in the rain, but he didn't seem to notice. "Then why? What did he offer you that would make it worth betraying her?"

"Nothing! He didn't give me anything. I didn't want to help him, but I didn't have a choice. He's my *father!*"

"That doesn't *mean* anything!"

Normally it didn't. Gods didn't really do the whole family thing because we were created, not born, so there were no genetic ties. Good thing, too, given all the incest. Labels like brother, sister, mother, father, didn't apply to us because that wasn't how we thought of each other. Persephone was weird. She'd been raised to believe she was human. Demeter and Persephone had the most human-looking mother/daughter relationship of all the gods.

Serious trust issues notwithstanding.

Hades advanced on me, and I edged backward. My heel caught on a branch. The branch snapped, twisting my foot out from under me. He darted forward. Screaming, I ducked my head away and thrust my hands toward him.

"Don't hurt me!"

"Give me one reason I shouldn't rip you limb from limb, you traitorous bitch."

I had thousands, but only one that would matter to him. "She wouldn't want you to."

Hades stopped. "*She* was the only one of us who gave a damn about you."

"I know." With a wary eye on him, I stood, keeping my movements slow and non-threatening. Not that Hades would ever feel threatened by me. He could crush me. And probably would before the day was through.

"Then why did you help him?" Hades grabbed me by the shoulders and gave me a rough shake. "Where is my wife?"

"Shouldn't you know?" They were married after all. Marriage between gods came with this whole power exchange thing, more mutually beneficial than fealty. They were supposed to be connected. You'd think that would come with a basic idea of each other's whereabouts.

Desperation danced across his face, and I suddenly understood. "You don't, do you? Zeus did something to mess with your connection, and that's how you got knocked out."

Hades worked a muscle in his jaw, and I knew I was right. No wonder he was freaking out.

"She's not dead," I assured him. Technically, a god getting enough worship to exist can't die, not even in combat, unless they're fighting their own kids, but that's a whole other story. Persephone hadn't come into her powers yet, so she fell into a gray area. "I saw her with Zeus. He must need her, Hades. He won't let her die. Otherwise, why bother taking her at all?"

He could, of course, maim, torture, and otherwise torment her, but I didn't think reminding Hades of that would do much good.

"Where is she?" Hades' voice was as tight as his grip. But he didn't look like he wanted to kill me anymore, so that was a plus.

"I don't know. And I *can't* help you find her. It's not that I want to help him, I just don't have a choice."

He stared at me for a minute, the words seeming to penetrate his rage. "Can't," he said finally. "Why not?"

Gods can't lie. So if a deity says they *can't* do something, you better pay attention.

"He's my father."

I could almost see the pieces click into place in Hades' head when shock, rage, and disgust flickered across his face in quick succession. It wasn't directed at me. Zeus made me an abomination by creating me without an ounce of free will. Even the Titans gave their children that much.

Hades let me go and stepped backward. "Can I trust you?"

I shook my head. "But I wish you could."

He closed his eyes. His entire body looked tense, desperate to be in motion, but something stopped him. After a minute that seemed to stretch out for all eternity, he sighed. "All right. Let's go tell Demeter."

"What good will that do?" I demanded, trying not to sound as hopeless as I felt. "Zeus is long gone from this realm. There's no stopping him now that he has her. You know she's going to break, and then he'll have access to this realm and the Underworld."

"I'm going to kill him."

I jerked my head up. He *couldn't* have just said that. Gods can't lie but . . . "That's not possible."

Hades opened his eyes and gave me a look so dark I got chills. "I'm well aware of the rules, Aphrodite. I was one of the six who decided which rules to keep and which ones to toss when we created these realms. It's time for them to be rewritten."

I gulped. So long as he had a majority of the original six to push the new reality through, he could rewrite the rules of creation. All to save one girl. Demeter would side with him because she would be as desperate to save Persephone as he was, and Hades could easily coerce Hera and Hestia into doing his bidding. Their souls were at his mercy.

But there was a balance. If he tipped it too far to one side . . . "You could unravel the world."

He didn't care. I could see that in his expression before the sentence even left my mouth. One of the most powerful deities in existence was an emotional wreck who wasn't thinking clearly.

For the first time I realized how dangerous Persephone was. There's a reason gods are so ambivalent about their children and that divine marriages are mostly political and not based on affection. Love is a human luxury. A being with the power to destroy everything with a word shouldn't place more value in one individual than the entire world, but Persephone had that effect on people. Zeus looked at her and saw power he could gain. Demeter loved Persephone with all the fierceness a mother could muster, and Hades. . . . Hades would break the world for her. She meant too much to too many people.

I had to find another way to kill Zeus.

And failing that—I hated myself for even thinking this—but remove her, and there was no threat. I'd have to kill Persephone.

Chapter VI

Persephone

ZEUS GRINNED. "Good morning, sweetheart."

Lashing out, I shoved him away from me and rolled out of bed, hitting the ground with a thud. I sprang to my feet. Pain washed over me, causing the room to swirl worse than a Van Gogh painting. Jaw clenched, I waited for the room to stop whipping around me, but when the room stopped spinning I discovered a whole new level of disorientation. There was no floor, no walls, no nothing. Through the trapped and hardened writhing gray mist beneath my feet, I could see a brilliant blue sky.

Swallowing hard, I took in the transparent, cavernous ceilings with a blink, keeping one eye on Zeus. How high in the air was I? Sunlight streamed through the walls of mist bathing the room in a strange gray-tinted light. This wasn't Olympus. The majestic mountain fell to the Underworld *way* before my time, but this place had the same feeling of awe-inspiring power.

"Nice place, huh?" His voice was smug.

Seriously? He'd hit me with lightning and taken me to . . . wherever the hell I was . . . and now he was fishing for a compliment? "Excessive. It is just you here, right?"

"For now, though eventually it will be home to all the gods. New Olympus, if you will." His hand stretched toward my face like he was going to touch my cheek or brush my hair out of my face or some other cliché skeevey-guy move. "You can stay here too if you give me what I want."

I smacked his hand away before he could touch me, unable to stomach the thought of Zeus ever putting his hands on me again. He looked hurt, of all things. *He's crazy,* I realized. *Completely certifiable, and I'm trapped here with him.*

"You don't have to be like that." Zeus kept moving closer, towering over me.

I inched backward. He followed, breaching my personal space, and stared into my eyes with terrifying intensity. Air hissed between my teeth as I drew in a sharp breath. The fact that I was inches away from a guy who could turn me into a living lightning rod had nothing to do with my fear. There was something frightening in the raw power of his gaze. A darkness. It swirled in their blue depths like fire and ice and rage. Meeting his gaze was like looking into the edge of the night, staring into the heart of a storm, or peering into the center of a supernova. I couldn't break away.

I'd forgotten. Gods help me, I'd spent so much time with my mom and Hades I'd forgotten what kind of power I was dealing with. He was the god king, ancient and forever. Zeus.

"We could have something, you and I." He moved closer. If his grin were any indication, he was getting off on this cruel game of cat and mouse. "You're not that bright, but you've got spirit." Zeus inclined his head, sweeping over every inch of me in a lingering once over. "I like that."

My back hit a wall, and I stifled a sob as he closed in on me. Zeus' body crushed mine against the cold wall of swirling mist. When he cupped my face, brushing the tears from my cheeks, I flinched away from him.

"This doesn't have to end in blood." His eyes locked to mine. Planting one hand beside me, Zeus allowed the other to travel down my arm, touch feather-light until he reached my hand and twined his fingers between mine. I faltered under the eternity of his gaze. I didn't have a chance against him. This was the god who imprisoned the Titans, brought forth all of creation, stood in the center of the universe, and watched time turn. What was I against that? I was . . .

I was . . .

I was quoting *Doctor Who*.

I broke free of his charm and shoved him off me. "Get out of my head."

Zeus slammed me into the wall, gripping the base of my neck with hands that crackled and sparked with electricity. My knee shot to his groin, but he sidestepped with ease. Electricity coursed through my veins.

With a wail, I collapsed. The misty floor swirled and churned beneath me as though agitated by his rage. My hands pressed against the floor on either side of his worn running shoes. Joel's shoes.

"That's more like it." His fingers wrapped in my hair, and he yanked my head up. "Shall we try again?"

I thought fast. "Xenia."

Zeus cocked his head, grip easing. "Xenia?"

"It's hospitality in Greek—"

"I know what it means," Zeus snapped. "But why are you bringing it up?"

"Showing kindness and hospitality to strangers from another land was so ingrained in Greek culture that even kings took in travelers off the street. The myths say you promised to always honor that code." Gods can't lie. It was a long shot, but anything was worth a try at this point.

Zeus snorted. His gold hair fell into his face, and he brushed it back in a gesture so reminiscent of Hades it hurt. "Daughters aren't guests. They're property."

I lifted my chin. "I am *not* your property."

"Oh, you're adorable." Zeus flicked his fingers, and a bolt of lightning shot down from the ceiling.

My screams ricocheted off the walls. He dragged me to my feet, a maniac gleam flashing in his eyes. "Swear fealty."

I gasped for breath, tears sizzling down my cheeks as my flesh began to heal. Trembling, I shook my head. The small motion almost knocked me out it hurt so badly.

Zeus steadied me. "Oh sweetheart," he murmured, gently brushing a strand of hair from my face. "I'm going to enjoy this."

When I heard the crackle of electricity going live in his hands, I squeezed my eyes shut. The lightning struck me again, and again, and again.

Chapter VII

Aphrodite

"WHAT DO YOU mean Zeus has her?" Demeter's eyes blazed so bright with fury it was amazing the small bridge Hades and I stood on didn't disintegrate. "You told me you'd keep her in the Underworld where she'd be safe."

The wooden bridge didn't feel like much protection against the angry goddess. I'd thought Hades was paranoid when he recommended we find neutral ground to break the news to Demeter that her daughter had been abducted. I was wrong. There wasn't much water beneath us, but with the air all around us, the lake below, and the earth on either side, we were in as neutral a territory as we could find outside of dreamscapes.

Demeter's gaze fell on me. "And what is *she* doing here?"

Hades stepped in front of me before Demeter could do any damage. "We were wrong. Joel was Zeus—"

"Joel is Zeus? *What?*"

Hades backtracked, bringing Demeter up to speed." . . . and when he created Aphrodite, he programmed her to follow orders." He shot me an apologetic glance that almost cancelled out the lingering rage on his face. Almost.

"Not just his," I interjected. "I'm loyal to all of my family to some degree, but I *have* to obey any family who outranks me. Including Persephone."

Hades' eyebrows shot up. "Persephone wouldn't control you."

"Uh, have you ever *met* your wife? She's bossy and—" I glanced between Hades and Demeter and cleared my throat. "Gosh, she's just a wonderful person. I'm sure she would have toned down the orders had she known I didn't have a choice in the matter."

"Joel is Zeus?" Demeter's shocked voice pulled the conversation back to its focus. I waited for Hades to make some sarcastic comment about Demeter not paying attention, but he remained silent, allowing her time to process the news, maybe? She didn't need it. "What else were you ordered to do?"

I squirmed under her piercing green eyes. She looked like a taller version of Persephone with the same blond hair, same tan, same build. But she had a coldness Persephone lacked. Something in her expression told me she would not only throw me to the wolves, but she'd watch them rip me apart with a smile on her face.

My mouth went dry, and I swallowed hard. "Nothing yet. But if I were you, I'd keep me supervised by someone who can't be charmed."

Demeter's hands shook. She took a deep breath, clenched her fists so tight her knuckles whitened, and glared at Hades. "*This*"—the venom in her voice had me edging backward—"is *your* fault."

"I'm aware of that." Hades' voice was flat, void of any emotion.

Demeter didn't care. "You brought that thing to *my* realm and put it under *my* roof with *my* daughter, and then you let Zeus—"

Let Zeus? I thought of Hades' crumpled body on the ground, the anguish in his eyes when he'd woken up and discovered her gone. She made it sound like he'd just handed Persephone over. My nails drummed on the wooden railing, and I looked over the glistening water. Somewhere between here and the path it had stopped raining, and the sun had emerged. Maybe it was a sign everything would be okay.

"I did *not* let him take her," Hades snapped. "If you weren't so stingy with your teleportation authorization, I'd have been able to get to her—"

Or maybe not. I glanced from Hades to Demeter, two of the oldest remaining gods in creation. Surely they could come up with a plan.

Well, a good plan. Hades hadn't mentioned anything about his whole "rewriting the rules" idea yet.

Demeter gasped. "Are you suggesting this is somehow *my* fault? *You* made her a target when you forced her to marry you—"

Forced? From what Melissa had explained, Hades married Persephone to rescue her from Boreas, the God of Winter. He'd saved her life.

"She was already a target! And thanks to you, she was helpless without any clue of what she was—"

I inspected my nails, but they didn't seem to notice or care how bored I'd grown. This could go on all day. "Really, the blame game's the most important thing on the agenda right now? Okay, I'll take a turn. This is your fault"—I gestured at Hades—"because you're an idiot. Had you treated her more like a goddess and less like an addlepated teenager, she wouldn't have given Joel a second look. Your marriage should have *made* her too powerful for Zeus to charm. Instead you left her weak. If you two were linked the way you should be, then you would have known about Thanatos and the Reapers.

"But don't look so smug," I added, turning to Demeter. "You'd have her believe she was nothing more than some silly mortal teenager. She shouldn't have been going on dates and hanging out with friends while there were demigods and minor deities going missing from your realm."

Demeter looked at me in surprise.

"Oh yes, I know all about that," I said with a condescending smile. "Did it ever occur to you she could help? That she *should*? You know"— I put a finger to my lip as a startling thought occurred to me—"the only person who treated her with the respect due to her station is Zeus. He at least treats her like a threat. You two"—I waved my hand—"seem to have forgotten she can actually be useful."

Demeter sucked in a breath like she was about to say something, but Hades cut her off. "We don't have time to argue about this right now. We need to rescue—"

"Rescue!" I threw my hands in the air, almost impaling a bright yellow butterfly that fluttered away on the breeze. "You still don't get it, do you? She's powerful! She ranks, and incidentally, she's part of a very small group that can kill Zeus. Use her."

Gods can't die. But everything has a weakness to keep balance and all that Zen crap. We're vulnerable to ourselves. An ingenious work around that still allowed for a balance, yet made us very difficult to kill because using our powers to hurt ourselves goes against our instincts. It would be like a human trying to gouge out his own eye. Every fiber of his being would rebel at the idea alone, forget acting on it.

But there was an unintended side effect to only being vulnerable to our own powers. Children. Gods pass powers onto their offspring. That power *can* be used against the god it came from, which meant that as Zeus' daughter, Persephone could kill him *without* breaking all of creation.

Demeter shook her head. "She's not strong enough."

I scoffed, propping myself up on the rail of the bridge overlooking the sparkling fountain. "Well then, let's fix that. I swear fealty—"

Hades' hand shot out, nearly knocking me off the bridge. "Stop. Persephone still hasn't come into her powers."

Which meant too much power could kill her. *Bingo*. I filed that tidbit of information away should the worst happen and I actually needed to use it. If there was one thing I had to work with, it was power.

Wait a minute! There's a reason there are no myths about child gods. Most gods are created full grown, like me, but a few deities want the experience of raising a child from infancy. Physically, a child's body isn't capable of channeling power until maturity. So child gods stay out of public eye, living off their parents' worship, until whatever random time their body decides it's ready. How was Persephone still alive? I'd felt her power. She had worshipers and at least enough power to put up *some* resistance to Zeus' charm.

Hades must be using the link to siphon off her extra power. I wasn't sure how often he had to do it, but surely she couldn't last too long without him.

Demeter sagged against the bridge as if all her hope had drained out of her. She must have come to the same conclusion I just had. Persephone was running out of time.

Hades closed his eyes. "We're going to find her."

"Maybe." I shrugged, not finding it likely, but saying so wouldn't help them right now. "But if you don't, and she's going to die anyway, why not take Zeus down with her?"

Chapter VIII

Hades

"CASSANDRA?" I pushed open the door to my throne room. Massive and carved from white marble, the room was more ostentatious than I liked, but it served its purpose. First impressions trumped personal preference. At the room's center stood two thrones cut from a solid black stone so dark they seemed to absorb all the light in the room. Pausing mid-stride, I stared, lost in thought. Was it just this morning Persephone and I'd sat there making plans to capture Aphrodite?

I shook off the memory, disappointed in myself. I'd been around since the beginning of creation, I should know better than to expect time to behave in a logical fashion. Time isn't consistent. Some minutes take hours and some days take years; others slip past so fast they're hardly experienced at all. Like last night. But every moment since her capture had lasted eons.

As much as I wanted to hit the ground running in my search for Persephone, I had an entire Underworld's worth of responsibilities. My realm never weighed so much. To spend any amount of time away, I needed to make arrangements. Cassandra was most likely already on it, but the Underworld had been through quite an upheaval with Thanatos' death. If I was going to be absent as well, no amount of prophecy could counter logistics.

Cassandra knelt beside a child in the opposite corner of the throne room with . . . everyone. I frowned. What matter would concern Cassandra, Moirae, Charon, Hypnos, *and* all the judges? When the door slammed shut behind me, Cassandra jumped to her feet, pushing the boy toward Minos. The child's eyes were blank with shock. He couldn't have been more than thirteen, far too young to earn a trip to my realm. Minos wrapped an arm around the child, obstructing all but his messy blond hair from my view.

"Get him settled, please, and then come right back," Cassandra instructed. Minos nodded, and not one, but all three of the judges escorted the child from the room, footsteps echoing off the high ceilings as their sandaled feet hit the marble floor.

Cassandra caught my quizzical look and shrugged. "Problems adjusting. You just missed the latest of the new souls. It would seem none of us are quite as good with people as you are."

That was an understatement. With any luck, Cassandra hadn't caused any psychological scarring with her "Yeah, you're dead, get over it" speech. She wasn't a people person. Ordinarily, I greeted the new souls and took special care to deal with any "adjustment problems." I enjoyed that part of my work. It was one of the few good deeds I could credit myself with. But as much as I'd love to tell myself otherwise, I wasn't settling in the souls out of the goodness of my heart. Just lack of better alternatives. The other gods had difficulties relating to humans. But those difficulties were nothing compared to the problems the humans in my court had relating to each other. Souls lose something the longer they're dead. They forget what it was like to worry, to be scared, to be human. Just yesterday, I'd caught Cassandra telling a frightened new soul I'd gone through a dark phase back when Dante passed through, but not to worry. I hadn't gone off my meds for centuries.

Fucking Dante.

Crossing the large room, I studied each member of my court as I walked. I'd done a lot of walking today. Of course I could have teleported within my realm, but I'd needed the time to think over the logistics of being gone and to close all but one guarded entrance into the Underworld. Demeter would post a guard on her side of the realm too, just in case.

It had taken too much time. Every minute I spent down here was a minute away from my search for Persephone and a minute longer she had to spend with Zeus. I knew what he wanted and what lengths he was willing to go through to get it. There was no more time to waste.

I paused at the obsidian throne. It was clear from Cassandra's face she already knew, and she would have wasted no time telling the others.

"Hades, I'm sorry." Charon's gray eyes were so full of concern I couldn't look at him straight on. I didn't have time to take solace in the presence of my friends. He looked down at his hands then returned his gaze to mine, all business. "What do you need us to do?"

Moirae, the current embodiment of the fates, and Hypnos, the god of sleep and the head of Underworld security, jumped in with condolences. I waved them away. "I need you all to cover things while I find her."

"Is that wise?" Cassandra leaned against the marble wall and gave me a frank look. "Being away from the Underworld right now?"

"No." I shoved my hair out of my face and narrowed my eyes at her, daring her to tell me to do otherwise. Pain racked through my entire body, and I knew what was causing it. Zeus was hurting her.

I had to find her.

Cassandra's thumbnail dug into the cuticle of her middle finger, leaving a white gouge where the living would bleed. She was nervous. The dead didn't handle stress well.

I took a deep breath to brace myself before asking my prophet the question that brought me down here. "Is she all right?"

She hesitated, twirling a strand of dark hair between two long fingers. "It's best I don't tell you."

"That bad?"

Her dark eyes met mine, begging me not to ask any more questions. "It will be."

Fury coursed through me, and I surged forward, opening my mouth to demand answers, then, with a herculean effort of will, swallowed my words. Cassandra didn't hedge. If it would help in any way, she would tell me because the future wasn't set in stone. I could still change it. But some prophecies had a tendency to self-fulfill. Sometimes the change that brought the vision about was the fact that someone knew about the prophecy in the first place. She'd been around long enough to know the difference.

I watched her for a moment. She fiddled with a strand of her dark hair, twirling it back and forth between her forefinger and thumb. That was a new nervous gesture. Whatever she'd seen . . . I didn't want to make it come true.

"Sit." I pushed aside my impatience and sat down, motioning for them to do the same. The chairs all faced the door. Damned inconvenient for speaking to one another. We didn't meet in here for more than issues between souls, but I didn't suggest we move to the dining room. Thanatos' absence was somehow more noticeable there.

Thanatos. My thoughts came to a screeching halt at the reminder of his betrayal. What could Zeus have offered him that made it worth turning his back on the Underworld? On us? Thanatos tricked Persephone into promising not to reveal he was working for Zeus and then tortured her for months, secure in the knowledge that she couldn't come to me for help.

Now Zeus had her. How had I failed so colossally at protecting her?

I'm not supposed to be your responsibility. The memory of Persephone's indignant voice echoed through my mind. She'd been right. Every time I stepped in, I made things worse. Rescuing her from Boreas painted an even bigger target on her back. I'd made Thanatos her guard. Then I'd all but hand-delivered her to Zeus when I encouraged her to see other people. Persephone would have been better off without my protection.

What if Aphrodite was right? Instead of putting all my focus on rescuing her, what if I gave Persephone the tools she needed to have a fighting chance? There were ways to trigger maturity. If one of her parents were to swear fealty to her and give her *every* drop of his powers, Persephone would come into hers. But how? The sheer power Persephone would need to charm Zeus into swearing over could kill her. It wasn't worth the risk.

A hand on my shoulder startled me out of my reverie. "Hades?" Cassandra's voice was gentle. "We've got this."

I blinked. "Right. I should . . ." I shifted, ready to stand, but Charon cleared his throat.

"She's lying, Hades, we're drowning without Reapers. We need more. Zachary and I didn't find that kid for . . . a while. We can't keep up with all the souls by ourselves. You know I wouldn't bring this up right now if the need wasn't great."

My mind flashed to the child with the empty eyes. Poor kid. Until a soul was released by a Reaper, it was stuck in its dead body, completely aware and helpless.

"Use the demigods." Reapers and demigods were the only souls that could come and go in the Underworld, thus they were the only potential spies. If Zeus had infiltrated as high as Thanatos, then no telling how many sources he had among them. I could take away a Reaper's power to cross between realms, but the ability was innate with demigods. If I couldn't control their abilities, I might as well use them.

"But Hades"—Moirae leaned forward, brown hair falling over her shoulders—"my visions are blind to demigods."

"Yes, thank you for stating the obvious." My already frayed patience snapped with such a violent surge of frustration that it even took me by surprise. I needed to be *done* with this so I could find her. Every minute I was down here . . .

I closed my eyes. Cassandra wouldn't tell me what was going to happen to her. If it was that bad . . .

I had to find her.

"We can rotate them in shifts," Hypnos suggested, adjusting the sleeves of his gray robes. "Keep them separated on the other side of the river when they're in our realm. Limit the information they could spread."

"They won't like that." Cassandra's dark eyes were narrowed in thought.

"They'll get over it!" I snapped.

She flinched, moving away from me with a small, almost imperceptible motion. "Of course. It's temporary, and there's enough that we can ask for volunteers."

It took a while, but eventually we got all the details hammered out. One by one I sent them away to complete their tasks until it was just Cassandra left in the throne room.

"Why didn't you tell me?" There was no chance Cassandra hadn't seen this coming with so many living deities involved.

She looked at the floor. "This has to happen, Hades."

For a moment, I was furious. How dare some human tell *me* what had to happen? Persephone was suffering, and Cassandra could have prevented all her pain with a single warning.

But the irony was too great for even me to ignore. I was a god. I'd allowed humans to suffer since their creation, sat by and watched while the rest of the pantheon used them as pawns in their petty games, and done nothing when my clairvoyants reported catastrophic happenings that would happen on the surface. There was so much I could have stopped. Instead, I'd felt good about myself for treating the souls in my realm well, like I was some sort of Prometheus figure. No wonder I struggled to sleep at night. But what else could I have done? Every hard decision I'd ever made, no matter how difficult, served the greater good.

I was intimately familiar with the greater good. It was cold and heartless and didn't give a damn about any of us. But we were all bound to it, because the only thing worse than being its agent was being its opposition.

Cassandra put a hand on mine, and I looked up, startled at the pain in her eyes. "I need you to trust me, Hades, without knowing why."

I nodded. "I do." I'd known Cassandra for lifetimes. She didn't have an ill-intentioned bone in her body. If she said this needed to happen, however hard that was to accept, it needed to happen.

Of course, I'd trusted Thanatos too. Right up to the moment I'd discovered he'd been torturing my wife and trying to turn my realm over to Zeus. Maybe I wasn't such a good judge of character after all.

"We're going to recruit as many of Zeus' offspring as we can," I told Cassandra, watching her face for a reaction.

She gave an impassive nod. "Who's left?"

"Ares, Apollo, Artemis," I listed off the names of Zeus' known children, frowning as I noticed a pattern. "A" names. No one expected Zeus to be an attentive parent, most gods weren't. But even in naming his children, he'd put as much distance between himself and them as possible. It was an unnatural indifference.

"That many?" Cassandra sounded surprised. "I knew about Apollo, but I assumed the rest had died."

"They all have charm, so it's not like they were going to run out of worshipers." I spoke without thought, my mind still distracted by the A to Z thing. Zeus had tried to prevent Athena from being born, Cronus style. She'd popped out of his head fully grown in the world's worst migraine, and he'd never again tried to prevent his children from being born. Instead he'd brought them into the center of power on Olympus. Not power, I realized, the center of attention. His demigods received a never-ending supply of quests or became key figures in epic wars. They all became heroes who died young.

"He's afraid of them," I realized. Zeus had kept them busy in the spotlight so he could always keep an eye on them without getting too close.

Cassandra gave me an odd look. "Of course he is. The Titans killed their parents, and then you all killed the Titans with him leading the way. History repeats itself. He's next."

Chapter IX

Persephone

"YOU KNOW WHAT I like about you?" Zeus' breath was hot in my ear as he stroked my scorched jawline. I'd lost count of how often he'd dragged me to my feet and propped me against this wall. He seemed to enjoy watching me fall into a crumpled heap of agony. "You never stop fighting. Even now you're scanning the room looking for something, a way out, a weapon, even though you know the truth. There is *nothing* here but me, you, and that." His eyes scanned my face for a reaction as he motioned over his shoulder at the bed.

I shuddered. He hadn't gone *there*, yet. Though what was stopping him I couldn't imagine. It wasn't as if I could put up much in the way of a fight, though gods knew I'd tried.

And tried, and tried.

My head lolled against the cool misty wall behind me, shoulders slumping in defeat. Zeus was right about me. I'd spent the last several unimaginably painful . . . hours? Days? Years? I didn't even know anymore, searching and fighting and trying to escape, convinced there *was* a way out of this. I just had to try hard enough to find it.

And I'd tried *so* hard.

Tears sizzled as they ran down my cheeks, tracing painful paths across my face before they dripped to the floor. What if there wasn't a—*No!* I wouldn't think that, I couldn't let myself, or I'd give in to him. Clenching my blackened knuckles, I made a fist and swung at Zeus' face. He fell for it, catching my arm with ease, and pinning it above my head with a grimace as the goo that had once been my flesh stuck to him. My other hand shot out, not at his face where he would see it coming, but at his kidney with as much force as I could muster.

He grunted, moving back just enough for me to break free of his grasp and make a beeline for the door. Lightning flashed, scorching the floor in front of me, and I scurried to the side. Zeus tackled me.

"You stupid bitch!" He grabbed me by the neck of my shirt, dragging my charred body across the misty floor until he reached that oh so familiar wall. Yanking me up so high my tiptoes barely brushed the surface of the floor, he pinned my arms above my head. I felt a flash of power and gasped as my hands passed through the wall. The frigid mist swirled, solidifying into a wall around my wrists.

I yanked against the bindings and lost my tenuous tiptoe hold against the ground. My feet slid out from under me, and I slammed against the wall, supported only by my wrists. Zeus stabilized me, hand turning bright with the blinding light of electricity, and he put it to my throat.

The human body was never meant to survive lightning. While Zeus held me under a steady stream of electricity, a myriad of things happened at once. In the last several however-long-it-had-been, I'd gotten past the intense and stunning pain enough to dissect each phase of agony.

First my muscles contracted, going rigid and stopping my heart while freezing me into place. Then I started to sweat. Sweat fueled the electrical current, causing more heat to build up in my body. Until I cooked. Heat built up, setting my blood boiling until any liquid within me became so pressurized that it burst free. That bit was excruciating, but it wasn't the worst part. No, that came later. Meanwhile, the electrical impulses that controlled my nervous system short circuited, sending conflicting and, of course, painful, messages to the brain.

For a while it seemed as if life were pain. Like nothing else had ever existed or would ever exist, making hope feel like a distant memory. Then came that blessed moment when I stopped feeling altogether, no pain, no thoughts, no hope, nothing. If I had a human body, that would be the point where I would die. Death is freedom. How had I never realized that until now?

But I'm not human, so something worse happened.

I started to heal.

Healing from a lightning strike at godspeed is exponentially more painful than the initial strike. My liquefied muscles re-knit.

Haltingly, my heart began its painful pump, faltering until my blood returned to its veins and capillaries, rebuilding the infrastructure of my body. Cooked flesh healed as my nerves roared back to life. Death would be a mercy. Hell, at this point I'd settle for loss of consciousness, anything to put a stop to the horrific pain. But Zeus was far too skilled to allow that to happen.

I screamed as another bolt hit me. Gods, it hurt! Electricity tore through my body like liquid fire, setting every vein and nerve ending aflame.

"Okay, okay!" I sobbed, collapsing against the wall. There was no way out. It didn't matter how hard I fought or how resourceful I was. The crushing hopelessness that accompanied that realization brought me to a point where I just couldn't take the pain anymore.

My head hung, and I stared at the bright blue sky beneath my feet. I twitched my fingers outside the misty wall, tantalized by the sky and the freedom it represented just beyond my reach. If only I could just drop through the floor and back to my realm.

"Do you have something to say?" Zeus' voice slithered through my ears, sending a shiver through me.

I nodded, tears chasing each other down my cheeks. *I'm so sorry, Hades.*

Hades couldn't hear me. Maybe equilibrium didn't cross realms? Or maybe Zeus had somehow burned away our connection. I took a deep, shuddering breath as I realized it was probably for the best that Hades couldn't see where my thoughts were headed. I'd wanted to be stronger than this. But torture was torture. And I was broken. After dealing with the Reapers for months, I'd thought I could handle anything, but Zeus put me through levels of anguish I hadn't known existed.

Calm washed over me as my body entered the blissful stage of non-feeling. Everything was going to be okay. Suddenly another bolt hit me, tearing through me and reawakening the pain. I couldn't even scream.

"I asked you a question," Zeus reminded me.

I couldn't take the pain anymore.

Chapter X

Aphrodite

MELISSA SIGHED, again. The sigh was loud, heavy, and brimming with irritation. I rolled my eyes, flipped to another page in my fashion magazine, and circled another picture.

Shooting me a dirty look, she tossed her brown hair over her shoulder with a huff. She sat on the floral-patterned comforter of Persephone's loft bed, as far from me as possible, with her knees drawn to her chest and her arms crossed over them. Melissa couldn't have looked more sullen if she'd tried. Gods, she probably *was* trying.

Melissa hated me. Oh sure, she'd deny it if I asked. After all, she did have that luxury. But her actions belied her words, conveying a hatred that ran almost as deep as the jealousy she so obviously suffered from. Whatever, I didn't like her either.

"How can you sit there and *read*"—her emphasis on the word made it clear how little she thought of my reading material—"while she's missing?"

I snapped the magazine closed and popped it on the wooden desk with enough force to stir every paper within five feet. "Your moping is no more helpful. They aren't going to find her any faster no matter what we do. So excuse me if I don't want to die of boredom while Persephone's gone."

I should have never suggested Demeter leave me with someone I couldn't charm. I'd forgotten my oath to never charm or allow harm to come to any of her priestesses. Especially Melissa the Teenage Bitch.

Melissa narrowed her eyes and muttered something under her breath. I clenched my teeth and picked up the magazine.

"I should be *doing* something." Melissa stared at her knees with so much intensity I worried they'd burst into flame. "Not babysitting you."

I closed the magazine again. "Do you think I like this any better than you do? My sole purpose for existing is to let Zeus use me as he pleases and to be nice to look at. Do you think that's fun? I hate him.

And despite that, all Zeus has to do is snap his fingers, and I'll stab my best, not to mention only, friend in the back. Sort of puts your tantrums into perspective, doesn't it?"

"Oh, shut up." Melissa's brown eyes flashed.

Melissa's mother, Demeter's head priestess, wanted Melissa to stay at the local university instead of going to Iowa State. Instead of getting mad at her mom, Melissa got pissed at Persephone. Humans are so irrational. Never mind that Persephone hadn't given a damn where Melissa went to school. Or that she'd made Melissa *immortal.* And sure, being a major deities' priestess should have been a huge honor, but Melissa would rather move to Iowa. She wanted to give up being second in command to an all-powerful deity for *school.* In Iowa! Oh yeah, and during all *that,* people in Athens were dropping dead like flies, and Zeus was hunting Persephone. Naturally Melissa decided that—you know what?—right then would be a great time to bring all that up. I guess she figured Persephone didn't have enough going on.

And people said *I* was an attention whore.

Treat her like you'd treat me, Persephone had instructed, unaware of course that I had to listen to what she said. Sitting quietly and being respectful while Melissa acted like a spoiled brat sucked. Fortunately I'd found a work around.

I got a whole lot more blunt with Persephone. Now I could say whatever I wanted.

"Yeah, I don't feel like shutting up. So I'm going to talk to you some more and because you're stuck with me, you're going to listen." Giving Melissa a malicious grin, I set the magazine on the desk. My smile faded and my voice went serious as anger I hadn't allowed myself to feel came simmering to the surface. "I am so sick of the whole lot of you whining about how bad you have it. It's a bit of a blow to the ego knowing that the world would actually be a better place if I didn't exist. But I manage. Every single person I know by name on this planet wishes I'd never been created. That Zeus could ask me to drop dead at any minute and I would *have* to comply is more than a little terrifying. Have I sat around moping about it? Nope. I've been doing something constructive with my time."

"Constructive?" Melissa snorted.

I threw the magazine at her. It hit her knees and flopped down on the bed. Melissa snatched it and held it up like she was about to throw it right back at me, but stopped when she noticed the pictures I'd circled.

"Look familiar?"

Melissa flipped the page and studied a picture of a completely hot guy modeling preppy clothes. He was the ultimate golden boy with his gold hair, skin, and eyes. All the markings of a demigod.

I walked to the door. Before my hand could so much as touch the doorknob, Melissa sprang up from the bed. "Where do you think you're going?"

I smirked, swinging the door open. "You wanted to do something so badly?"

"You're supposed to stay here."

"And you're supposed to babysit. Coming?"

Chapter XI

Hades

AFTER MY DISCOURAGING chat with Cassandra, I teleported to the Elysian Fields. I didn't spend a lot of time here. For the most part, Elysium was filled with the best of the souls. Those who had done great good in their lives. But it was also home to deceased deities. Olympus stood over the bright sunny fields and meadows. Most souls felt the vibrant purple mountain added beauty to the perfect landscape. I disagreed.

Olympus cut a dark shadow across perfection, serving as a reminder that there was no place untouched by evil in all of creation. I loathed Olympus. Everything changed the moment this mountain towered over my life. We had become what we'd worked so hard to defeat, perhaps not as bad as the Titans, but this mountain elevated us to gods, scowling down at all of creation.

Yet it was in my Underworld. The fall of Olympus had been the final harbinger of the death of the gods. I could have incinerated the blasted mountain the moment it came down or left it to rot in Demeter's realm. But it meant something to *them*, and they'd lost enough.

Gods, nymphs, and dozens of other extinct creatures stopped what they were doing to watch me approach the palace. I didn't come here often. Still, I didn't hesitate when I walked through the columns. This was *my* realm.

"Wow, two visits in one century." Hera moved between the sand-colored columns with an inhuman grace. There were no walls here, only columns stretching an impossible distance into the air, holding up a very tall, very flat slab of stone ceiling. It couldn't have been more different from my palace. That wasn't a coincidence.

"I'm almost flattered." Hera's curly brown hair was piled on the top of her head in an archaic Roman style. She wore a violet chiton. I hadn't seen one of those shift-like dresses since the hydra still plagued Ancient Greece. Some people didn't know how to move on.

"Thinks the man in the cape." Hera let out a throaty chuckle at my surprised look. "I can always tell what you're thinking, Hades. Such an open book."

"You're the only one who ever thought so." I sat on one of the tall backless couches.

Her lips turned up in a mysterious smile. "Maybe it's not so much an open book as a mirror. Perhaps we're both just damaged beyond repair." She sat beside me on the couch, fingers trailing over the narrow strip of white upholstery between us. "What can I do for you?"

"Your husband has taken my wife. Do you have any idea where?"

She tilted her head and put a hand on my shoulder. "Poor Hades, will you ever find someone who deserves you?"

I removed her hand from my shoulder with a bit more force than necessary. "It wasn't consensual."

"Isn't that your working theory on what happened to me? That I was charmed." Her gray eyes bored into mine. "You want so badly for me to be a victim. Did you ever stop and wonder if maybe I just don't love you?"

I ignored her use of the present tense. "At the time it was easier to assume you weren't an opportunistic bitch," I replied calmly. "I'm not here about you. I'm trying to find her, and you haven't answered my question."

"Do you love her?" Jealousy flamed to life in Hera's eyes.

"Exclusively. You still haven't answered me. Where would Zeus keep her?"

She kept her gaze locked with mine as though she were trying to unnerve me with her proximity. "What makes you think I would know?"

I took a measured breath. What I wanted to do was threaten to throw her into Tartarus until she remembered how to answer questions. But Hera fed on anger like most people breathe air. If I snapped, she'd be in control. Hera had controlled enough of my life.

"You were many things, Hera, but oblivious was never one of them."

Hera's gaze went hard. "Zeus and I didn't exactly have pillow talks. If you'll recall, he sucked the life from me and threw me down a mountain the moment I outlived my usefulness."

"What I recall is you bringing down the mountain with you and single handedly ending the era of Olympus."

Hera's eyebrows rose and her lips pursed into an "O" shape.

"What?" I asked. "You thought it escaped my notice that Olympus' fall coincided with your demise? I was around when you created this abomination. I remembered some of your . . . unusual design flaws. You're the one who did all the marketing, too. When the mortals saw Olympus fall, they thought it meant the gods had died. So the gods did."

"You've always paid entirely too much attention to me."

"And you always sucked at answering questions. Where would Zeus keep my wife, Hera?"

"To keep her from you?" Hera smiled. "As far out of your reach as possible. Beyond that, I haven't the faintest idea."

I clenched my teeth to keep from cursing.

"But I know of someone who's always kept excellent tabs on him."

"And who's that?"

"My firstborn."

Athena. Demeter would know where to find her. I rose from the couch to go, then paused. As much as I hated to ask Hera any more questions, she was the only god I knew of who would know the answer.

"After you married, were there ever times you couldn't sense him?"

Hera frowned. "What do you mean?"

"Marriage, it's unbreakable, right? He couldn't—"

She laughed. "Come now, Hades, you know the answer to that. Nothing is unbreakable." I waited through Hera's dramatic pause. "You can always kill her."

I rolled my eyes. "I meant from an outside source. Zeus hit her with lightning and it knocked me out. I haven't heard her since."

"Knocked *you* out?"

I waved away her surprise. "Yeah, I know. I always thought sympathy bonds were a myth, but apparently they come with equilibrium."

"Equilibrium?" Hera didn't seem amused anymore. "With that infant?" She paused as if giving me time to object to her description. I refused to rise to the bait. Fluttering her eyelashes with a dramatic sigh, Hera responded, "Not possible. You'd know right away if you could feel *everything* she was feeling."

"Maybe we can only feel extremes. He hit her with lightning, Hera."

She fell silent, digesting this. "She's still a baby, isn't she? I suppose it's possible he could have killed her."

I shook my head, unwilling to consider the possibility. "He still needs her. Besides, if she were dead she'd be down here."

"Doesn't she have Thanatos' power?" Hera asked, referring to the god of death Persephone had recently charmed to death. "If she swears fealty to Zeus, he could keep hold of her soul. He wants you to waste your time looking for her. What makes you think he doesn't already have what he wants? Really, Hades, she's a child. How long do you expect her to stand up to Zeus' torture? Look on the bright side, this way Zeus can't use her to kill you."

"To kill *me?*" I barked an incredulous laugh. "That's not going to happen."

Hera's face turned puzzled then crafty. "You don't know."

"Of course I *know*." As if I would have married Persephone without knowing all the risks.

"She's a part of you, Hades, and you're a part of her. You exchanged power to get married." Hera ran her tongue over her top teeth. "She could kill you, but it doesn't matter. If you can't sense her, she's dead. And if by some miracle she's not, you should probably transfer enough power her way to put her out of her misery. Otherwise Zeus will have access to your realm and your head on a silver platter."

Persephone wouldn't do that. I could see her breaking and swearing fealty to Zeus. All that would take was a second of weakness and the words would be spoken, but for her to physically attack me? Unlikely.

Not that it mattered, if she pulled a Boreas and swore *everything* to Zeus, he'd inherit the ability to kill me.

But he'd still have to face me to do it.

"Do you think I want him to win?" Hera asked, pulling me from my thoughts. "Hades, I have nothing left to gain. And you have a responsibility to this realm to eliminate *any* threat. Even her."

Out of the question. But I could change the rules, make up down, and black white. I could strip Zeus of his powers. Hell, I could make him allergic to water if I wanted.

I'd spoken to Hestia. She hadn't been happy but she'd agreed so long as I promised it was a last resort.

Hera read the thoughts on my face. "No."

"I could make your stay here *much* less comfortable," I reminded her.

Hera looked at me then. *Really* looked at me in that way that felt like she was looking through me and weighing my every thought and intention. Whatever she saw must have terrified her because the blood drained from her face.

"Okay," she whispered, visibly shaken. "I'll help reset the rules when you ask me to."

I nodded and turned to leave, then paused when I remembered the flash of jealousy in her eyes when she'd asked if I loved Persephone. I'd seen that look before. So had Minthe and Laurel, two women I'd once cared for who Hera turned into plants so even their souls would remain out of my reach.

"I assume this goes without saying, but if you or any of yours so much as look in my wife's direction with ill intent, I will end your existence."

"Haha," she said dryly, but I heard the fear in her voice.

"You think I'm kidding? Aren't you curious why Thanatos didn't end up here after going after Persephone?" I turned, met her eyes, and let her mull that over.

"I'll bite. Why?"

"I shattered his soul."

Chapter XII

Persephone

"YOU WERE SAYING?" If Zeus' stifled yawn were any indication, he was bored. The metal folding chair he'd summoned looked completely out of place in his misty palace. He straddled it, one arm dangling over the back.

"I—" The words wouldn't come. I tried again. "I—"

"What did I tell you about stalling?" Zeus raised his hand, electricity flickering between his fingers.

"No!" I screamed as the lightning hit me again. My flesh sizzled and cooked like bacon. A bright light seared my eyes and then pain hit me, immeasurable pain, as my body knit back together.

"I—" I tried again, desperate, but the words wouldn't come. Frustrated tears sizzled on my face. This wasn't fair. I was ready for this to end! I was willing to give up everything! Why couldn't I swear fealty to him?

My mind flashed back to when I'd almost charmed Hades into swearing fealty to me. That was when I figured out that Zeus had been controlling me.

"*I won't do it!*" I'd screamed to Aphrodite back when I thought she might be Zeus in disguise. "*I won't be used against him. Never. I will never charm him! I will never act with the intention of hurting him! You can't make me!*"

Laughter bubbled up in my throat, high pitched and hysterical, bitter with the taste of tears. This was just too good. I'd been tortured for months because of a promise I made to Thanatos, but it was all worth it now because that same stupid divine technicality was going to keep Zeus from winning. Here I'd always thought of the inability to lie as a weakness. Now it was my weapon.

I *couldn't* swear fealty to Zeus because I couldn't betray Hades! Relief flowed through me in joyous waves. Giving Zeus access to the Underworld would cause more harm to Hades than anything else I could ever do. No matter what Zeus did to me, I couldn't swear.

Oh gods, it didn't matter what Zeus did to me. He'd never stop. Oh gods. This was never going to end. The relief turned to dread and settled in my stomach like a rock. I was never getting out of this. Hades would have come for me by now if he knew where to find me, and as much as I balked at the fact that I *needed* to be rescued, I couldn't escape on my own. Without the ability to swear fealty, I had no way out.

But maybe that was a good thing. Zeus didn't know I *couldn't* swear, so he'd waste time trying to get me to crack. "I will never tell Zeus why." Whispering the soft oath beneath my breath bound me to it for better or worse. If he learned why I couldn't swear fealty to him, he'd find another way to gain access to my realms. Maybe I couldn't fight Zeus, but I could buy time for those who could. Hades . . .

This was bigger than me, bigger than Hades. This was about everyone who lived in Mom's realm and the Underworld. Every single being who would ever or had ever lived. Zeus was insane, and it was my responsibility to protect my people, whatever the cost to me.

And it was going to cost a lot. The second of clarity, coupled with the realization I'd just signed myself up for unending torture, fractured my already traumatized mind. Something snapped. My laughter bounced off the walls, eerie and maniacal. Zeus muttered something about taking it too far, and stood up, approaching me with wary eyes.

"Goodnight, sweetheart," Zeus murmured. "I think you've had enough for today." He touched my head, and before I realized what was happening, a current of electricity surged through me.

Goodnight indeed.

Chapter XIII

Aphrodite

"I SHOULD BE DRIVING," I insisted for what seemed like the hundredth time.

Melissa tossed her brown hair over her shoulder and checked the rearview mirror before changing lanes. "I'm the babysitter. I drive."

Flipping down the visor, I examined my hair in the mirror, but when I locked gazes with myself, I was struck by a thought. Could I charm myself? I had enough control to avoid stupid mistakes. But only because Persephone had found me and trained me. What if she hadn't? I stared into the mirror and pushed a little charm at it, watching my aquamarine eyes for any reaction. Nothing.

Good. I flipped the visor back up and turned my attention to Melissa. "You get that if we get pulled over in this stolen car, I'm the one who can charm the police officer into looking the other way, right?"

"You can charm him just fine from the passenger seat."

"You really don't have an issue with me using charm?" I don't know why I was surprised. She hadn't objected to me charming our way aboard the flight to Miami or the subsequent paperless car rental.

Melissa shot me a condescending look. "I'm her best friend, not her carbon copy."

I fell silent, considering that.

"You shouldn't make fun of her, you know," Melissa added. "If she didn't have the moral high ground, Hades would have thrown you into Tartarus the moment he first saw you."

Not technically. I'd be in a sub-realm just outside of Tartarus. But it still wouldn't be fun.

"And she'd be better off." I double checked the blue dot that marked our location on Melissa's phone. It moved at a slow crawl down Ocean Drive.

Finding a model from a photo in a magazine was hard. Even with charm. We'd spent most of yesterday tracking down the information we could glean from the ad. The model's name was Adonis, and he lived in Miami. So we hopped on a plane at the Atlanta airport and spent the rest of the evening running around random offices in downtown Miami. *Then* Melissa had the brilliant idea to run a search for him on social networks.

Adonis had some serious stalkers.

Lucky for us, Adonis had a photo shoot scheduled bright and early this morning on Miami Beach.

"You can't really think that." Melissa's brown eyes were wide.

I blinked, retracing the conversation to remember what she was talking about. "I'm grateful they helped me. But she would have been better off with me safely out of the way."

Melissa turned on her blinker and eased into a parking lot. I flashed a smile at the lot attendant, and he waved away Melissa's money. "Is that why you're being so helpful? You feel guilty?"

I shook my head. "Don't be naive. I benefit more from Zeus' death than anyone."

Now it was her turn to fall silent. She turned off the car and stretched before she took off her seatbelt and reached into the backseat for her purse. "Well . . . what's the plan?"

"I charm Adonis and bring him back to Demeter's."

"They aren't going to be happy with us. My mom will probably kill me when she finds out where we've been."

My fingers fell off the handle of the car door, and I whipped around so fast I felt muscles in my neck give. But Melissa only looked pleased with herself, as if driving her mother to murder were the ultimate teenage goal. I rubbed my neck, scowling. Stupid humans and their exaggerations. She burst into laughter.

"You thought I was serious? She'd have to notice we were gone to kill me." Melissa shut the car door with more force than required, and I stepped out of the car, shading my eyes in the bright sunlight.

We didn't have to walk long before we found the photo shoot. A girl with messy hair adjusted a light board and shouted instructions, while a man with thick glasses snapped pictures. Four half-dressed blondes frolicked in the sand in some sort of pretend volleyball game. In the center of the commotion was Adonis.

Looking at him set my heart racing. He was perfect. His golden features shone like the sun. A rakish grin lit up his face, and his unbuttoned shirt billowed in the wind, revealing an impressive six-pack.

"Thank you, wind," Melissa whispered beside me.

Bobbing my head up and down in agreement, I admired the model. Wow! Wait a minute, what in the hell was I doing gawking at a demigod like a deranged nymph? I snapped out of it and straightened up, tossed my hair behind my shoulder, and turned on my charm full blast before striding across the beach.

"Whoa!" One of the male models gasped.

I felt the weight of everyone's eyes on me and reveled in the reverence of their slack-jawed expressions. This was more like it.

"Come with me." I didn't wait for Adonis to acknowledge the order, but turned on my heel, confident he would follow.

He didn't.

I turned, pouring more charm into my gaze. "Come. With. Me."

"Why?" he asked, completely unaffected by my charm.

"Because I said so," I sputtered, bewildered by his indifference.

He raised an eyebrow. "You seem to have a rather high opinion of yourself, so I'll try to break this to you gently." Leaning toward me, he put a hand on my shoulder and stage whispered, "You aren't as impressive as you think you are."

Melissa giggled. Adonis looked up as if noticing her for the first time, easy grin faltering. "Can I give you some advice, or are you so brainwashed by this thing that you can't understand me?"

Melissa giggled again. "I'm not charmed, if that's what you're asking." She blinked and looked around at the other models and photographers. They stared back at her, expressions blank.

"They won't remember this conversation," I assured her.

Adonis narrowed his eyes. "Stop charming them."

"It's for their own good," Melissa murmured. "If they tell anyone about this or mention the gods—"

"They aren't stupid!" Adonis snapped. "Unlike you, hanging around these creatures willingly. If you were smart you'd stay away because whatever they've promised you isn't worth it."

"Excuse me?" I demanded.

Melissa grinned at Adonis as if she'd discovered the one person in the whole of creation who felt the same way she did. "I don't like them either, but you may want to listen to this one. She's trying to save your life."

"Come along, Melissa. He's not worth the effort."

"Save me from what?"

I smirked at Adonis and opened my mouth to tell him off, but Melissa spoke first.

"Zeus is killing off all his kids, including demigods."

"What makes you so sure Zeus is my father?"

"You have charm," I interrupted. "Not controlled of course, but charm only comes from Zeus."

"Is that why he's immune to you?" Melissa asked in an undertone.

I shook my head. "That happens every now and then, random fluke of the fates. The gods can't touch him."

Melissa's eyebrows shot up. She started to say something, but I cut her off with a glare.

The look on Adonis' face told me his parentage was news to him. That wasn't uncommon. Most demigods knew they were demigods. It was obvious to anyone in the know thanks to their distinctive physical features, but few knew which god spawned them. Gods were fond of disguises.

"I thought Zeus was dead."

"Not yet." I gave him a dark smile. "But I'm sure he'll be around to explain soon enough. Bye now."

I flounced off, dragging Melissa behind me.

"Wait!" he called.

I turned, feigning indifference. "Yes?"

He hesitated and looked at Melissa. "Can I trust you?"

"Me?" She drew back in surprise.

He smiled at her. "Well, I know I can't trust *her*."

I narrowed my eyes and studied Adonis closely, something akin to dread growing in my stomach. Demeter had been tracking, warning, and hiding demigods for months. Yet somehow she'd missed the one featured in Persephone's magazines?

I should have talked to her before we left. But I'd been so eager to do something helpful, to prove to myself I had at least a little free will, that I'd rushed off and dragged Melissa with me.

"You can trust us," Melissa promised.

But could we trust him?

Chapter XIV

Hades

I STUDIED THE map of the University of Georgia's campus, searching for the Philosophy department that Athena headed. This place was more complex than the entire Underworld. I grimaced and glared at the map as if I could force it to give me answers. A never-ending river of noisy students flowed around me, and the sun battled against the black pavement to determine who could throw off the most heat.

Across the street, a gardener tended to a Weeping Willow with a trunk nearly as thick as he was. I averted my eyes, swatting at a mosquito that dared bite my neck. Why did so many gods live in Georgia? If I were stuck on the surface, I'd find a less humid place with fewer hills. I'd been back and forth around this stretch of buildings for ten minutes, and somehow, it managed to be uphill both ways.

"You look lost." A spiky-haired brunette separated from the mass of students and looked me up and down. She fiddled with the strap of her backpack, and her freckled face turned pink. "Where are you headed?"

"Peabody Hall." I showed her the map.

"A man willing to ask for directions? Nice!" She flashed me a grin and pressed a button on her phone and checked the time. "I can take you."

I grinned. "You sure? I'd hate to make you late to class."

She looked me over again. "Worth it." Her eyes widened like she couldn't believe she'd said that out loud. Turning on her heel, she coughed, clearing her throat. "This way."

The girl was named Kristen, a sophomore who was studying to be a social worker. She worked at a place called Barberitos and was off tonight if I wanted to grab a cup of coffee at the Two Story Coffee House.

"No, thanks," I said without explanation.

Her face fell. "Not a coffee drinker? We could go get something stronger. Ever been to Trapeze?"

"No, I like coffee." I glanced at the map. Were we going the right way? I looked up to ask and noticed her glum expression, then thought over our conversation and sighed, hearing the unintentional, unspoken qualifier. *Just not with you.* Damn. I was normally good at human interaction. Then again, the dead weren't all that flirtatious, so this was new territory for me. "It's not . . ." I hesitated. "You seem nice."

Kristen brightened.

"But I'm married."

Her eyebrows shot up, and she glanced at my left hand. "I don't see a ring. Oh wow, I actually just said that out loud." Her face colored. "Uh, um . . . My sister didn't do the ring thing either. She told her fiancé she'd rather they spend the money on traveling somewhere cool."

What did rings have to do with anything? *Right.* Humans and their marketing traditions. Some Greek idiot believed the ring finger on the left hand had an artery that led straight to the heart. And they bought it. How such an intelligent species could be so uninformed about their own physiology for so much of their existence was beyond me. Humans scoffed at the idea of gods and turned their backs on us, leaving us all to die. Yet some ridiculous notion that wearing a chunk of metal on a certain finger bound two souls until death stuck. Figures.

Wait a minute, should I have given Persephone a ring?

"This is it," Kristen announced, startling me out of my reverie. I jerked my head up, surprised by the sudden appearance of a brick building. She pulled a notebook out of her backpack and scrawled a number onto a piece of paper. "In case you change your mind."

Ignoring the piece of paper, I thanked her and climbed the stone stairs. The heavy wooden door thudded closed behind me as I scanned the room numbers for Athena's lecture hall. Her room was packed. I slipped in with a group of students who somehow managed to look studious and sloppy at the same time. Athena's back was turned while she wrote on the board. Very little conversation buzzed around me while I found a seat in the back and settled in. The students near me didn't talk or look at each other much. Instead, they all had their heads bowed over their desks as they stared down at their laps with laser-like intensity.

I frowned, wondering what kind of class Athena was teaching when the boy next to me solved the mystery.

"Classic." He spoke with a slow drawl, seemingly unbothered by the greasy chunk of dark hair hanging in his eyes. He flicked his gaze from me to the board. "You've read it, right?"

I must have looked confused because he drew his cell phone from beneath his desk and waved it at the board.

I glanced at what Athena had written.

Do androids dream of electric sheep?

His fingers moved across the screen of his phone. "She posted it on ELC this morning, so you should be able to download it." The boy started to add more but stopped when Athena turned to face the class.

"What does it mean to be human?" Athena asked. The entire room fell silent. Heads popped up, looked at her straight on, every eye glazed over with reverence. Subtle waves of charm washed through the room, commanding attention, drawing their worship, and likely opening their minds to her lecture. I couldn't decide if I was disgusted or impressed. I'd never liked charm, but this seemed like a good use of it. The students hung on her every word, open, engaged, and learning. So long as Athena taught halfway decent material, this was one of the more mutually beneficial uses of charm I'd ever seen.

Athena hadn't changed since the last time I saw her. She tucked her carefully coiffed brown hair behind her ear and looked out at the class with emotionless gray eyes. "We'll talk theories in a moment, but I'd like to know your opinions. What makes you human? What makes you different from every other creature out there?"

"We can think?" a boy wearing a loose button up shirt and khakis called from the front row.

"We have emotions?" a girl asked, pushing her glasses up the bridge of her nose with her pinkie.

"We're self-aware? Like, we think about thinking and time and stuff?"

Gods, when had college kids become so uncertain? All their replies ended with an upward lilt like they were asking a question instead of supplying an answer.

After a couple of students gave faltering answers, I called from the back of the room, voice strong and certain, "They can lie."

Athena jerked her head toward me, panic flashing in her eyes as she scanned the rows of students. When her gaze locked on mine, the color drained from her face. "Class dismissed."

The students looked at her in confusion. Athena didn't look away from me, but her voice took on a panicked edge. "Get out, now." Her charm was in full effect.

The room filled with noise. Chairs scraped across the blue carpet as they were pushed back from the desks. Papers rustled as they were gathered and shoved into folders. Hushed whispers whipped around me as the students filed out of the classroom. A few glanced my way.

I stretched my legs and folded my arms over my chest. When the last student left, I curled my lips in a grin. "Philosophy?"

"I didn't know about Zeus. I didn't."

"You know about him now. Did your message get lost in transit, or did you have the impression I wouldn't be interested in the news?" I could see her pulse pounding in her neck.

Athena pressed her elbows to her sides like she was trying to make herself smaller, less threatening. All she accomplished was wrinkling her gray power suit.

"Where is he, Athena?"

Her chin trembled. "I don't know."

I unfolded myself from the tiny desk and stood, keeping my stance casual, then walked through the row of desks. Athena tensed. She looked ready to run. Sticking my hands in my pockets, I stopped at the edge of the first row, leaving her the front of the room.

She inched away until her back met the white board. "All I have are theories."

"I'm going to need more than theories."

Chapter XV

Persephone

"PERSEPHONE."

My eyes fluttered open. *Hades*. It was his voice. My vision blurred then focused. He knelt in front of me, his eyes marred with dark lines of worry.

"You're here." I threw my arms around him.

His lips found mine and he kissed me, pulling me to my feet.

"How are you here?" I asked, breaking off the kiss. My head was pounding and the room swirled around me in indistinct colors. I swayed on my feet, and his grip on me tightened.

"You're dreaming."

"Right." Closing my eyes against the crushing disappointment, I leaned into Hades, drawing on his strength as that spark of hope sputtered and died. Of course it was just a dream. Dreamwalking was one of many forms of communication the gods could use. I sucked at it, which explained the room swirlies.

"I don't know how long we've got until you wake up." His voice was urgent. "Persephone . . . Did you—"

"No." I slid my necklace back and forth on the chain and started to explain how I couldn't swear fealty, but Hades interrupted me.

"I have a plan."

All my worry fell away. Yes, this situation was bad, but Hades would find me. Yeah, it would be better to save myself, but I was in over my head here. He could fix this. "I knew you were going to get me out of here."

Hades looked down. When his dark hair fell into his face, I pushed it off his forehead. He jerked his head up, seeming surprised, then closed his eyes and shook his head. "I can't promise that, but . . ." He hesitated and fumbled for my hands.

Looking down at our entwined fingers, I frowned. There was something . . .

"Do you trust me?" His voice was subdued, as if he weren't sure how I would answer.

I looked up at him. "Of course." I trusted Hades absolutely.

"If you swear fealty to me, then you can't swear to him. It's not a perfect plan . . . But . . . "

I frowned. "Will that work? Thanatos swore fealty to me after he swore fealty to Zeus."

Hades' thumb moved back and forth on mine. "That's different. You and Zeus are in the same bloodline."

I stared at our hands, a feeling of unease creeping through me. "Why can't I hear you?"

"What?"

"In my head, you said once we hit equilibrium—"

"Persephone, this is really important."

I pulled my hand out of his grip. Annoyance flickered over Hades' face, so I moved away from him, unnerved. "Why can't I hear you?"

A muscle twitched in his jaw. "Maybe it was the lightning?"

"Is it permanent?" Voice quavering, I fiddled with my necklace. "I couldn't even hear you when we kissed. That . . . I mean . . . We've always—Did it sever everything? I mean, are we even still married?"

Hades drew back, looking surprised. "I've never heard of anything breaking a marriage like that."

At least the idea seemed to worry him, too. I was painfully aware of the fact that Hades only married me to save my life. It was supposed to be permanent, but if it wasn't . . . would he *want* to marry me again? Even if he did, would he insist on waiting until I was older or some other nonsense? We'd *just* gotten over the age debate. If it started again . . .

"Persephone." His voice was gentle. "This is really important. If the marriage still holds, then Zeus can use you to get into the Underworld. The Underworld needs to be protected. We can figure everything else out later." He gripped my hand again. "Please?"

His grip felt wrong. It was like our hands didn't know each other. Most of the time, when Hades and I held hands, it felt natural, like he was an extension of me. I looked up and met his eyes. "You want me to swear fealty to you?"

He nodded.

"So . . . What do I do, just say your name and—"

"Nothing formal. Just telling me you swear fealty is enough."

I pursed my lips. "If we're not married anymore, I'm pretty much useless to Zeus, right?"

He seemed to consider. "Zeus is still after your mother's realm."

"Is he?" I stood and put some distance between us.

"You seem remarkably unconcerned about this." Hades' voice was tight with anger.

"And you seem remarkably unconcerned about me. Not even going to ask if I'm okay, Hades?"

Surprise flashed in his eyes, but not regret. "Are you okay?"

I shook my head. "No."

He sighed. "Persephone, I'm sorry. I know this is a lot, but I really need you to—"

I walked farther away. "You're not Hades."

He sneered. "You're pathetic. You should have been left to Boreas. You've been nothing but trouble. Do you honestly think you're worth it?"

I glared at Zeus. He knew that I knew, but he was trying to make it hurt more. If everything went his way, I'd never see Hades again. I refused to let this be the last thing I remembered of him.

"You're a novelty. A goddess who acts human. But you'll outgrow that and then what will you be? Do you really think you can compare to Hera? I've been with nymphs who have more depth than you. You . . . "

Adios, I thought. Nothing happened.

I frowned. That should have booted him out of my head and closed it to visitors.

Maybe it didn't work if you were knocked out? I did my best to ignore him. But that didn't stop him from talking.

And talking.

And talking.

I ignored him, or tried to. Squeezing my eyes shut, I tried to force myself into a deeper dreamless sleep by sheer force of will. I failed. And he kept on talking. Threatening.

Over the next few days, we fell into a routine of sorts. I'd wake up, and he'd torture me until I hit my breaking point. Then he'd knock me out before I could close my mind, and he'd wear different faces, mostly Hades, sometimes my mom. And he'd talk.

Constantly.

Saying terrible things. Things Hades would never say to me.

The words cut me like knives, but they also brought me a twisted sense of joy. As long as he was spending every spare moment trying to break me, he wasn't watching them.

Chapter XVI

Aphrodite

DEMETER'S HOUSE was full of Muses, minor deities, and priestesses when Melissa, Adonis, and I got back. Her house wasn't small, but it wasn't built to be a conference hall either. Blinking, I tried to take them all in. Deities crowded on and around the sectional sofa, perched on the hearth of the fireplace, and sat on the wooden stairs leading up to the bedrooms. My head spun trying to match all the names with faces. I didn't realize there were so many gods left. A priestess on her way out of the kitchen with a tray of finger foods tripped over a god—Thalia, I thought—lounging on the bottom step.

"Oh good!" Melissa's mother, Minthe, hurried out of the kitchen, dodging the off-balance priestess with aplomb. She wore a white apron with red flowers on it. If I never saw floral patterns again, it would be too soon. Good gods, the thing had ruffles. "I was just about to go looking for you."

Beside me, Melissa attempted a contrite expression but didn't quite pull it off. She still looked entirely too happy about getting into trouble.

But come to think of it, Mrs. Minthe didn't seem nearly upset enough. She looked relieved. And not, "yay, my daughter's alive. I don't have to file a missing persons report" relieved. Just "ooh, an extra set of hands" relieved.

"Can you grab the nice plates? You know, the ones in the box downstairs?"

Melissa tilted her head in confusion. "Don't you want to know where I've been? What I've been doing?"

Now it was Minthe's turn to look puzzled. "Did you leave?" An oven beeped in the kitchen, pulling the already distracted priestesses' attention off her errant daughter. "Oh! I'll just—" She moved toward the oven, looking more frazzled than concerned. "Uh, the nice plates, okay? You know the ones?"

Melissa nodded, looking shell-shocked. "Excuse me," she murmured, stomping off toward the basement door. She threw it open with so much force it crashed into the horn Pan kept strapped to his back. "Sorry."

I heard her foot hit every single step down to the basement.

"Would you like one?" Laurel, one of Demeter's priestesses, asked.

"What?" I looked at the woman and then noticed the platter she carried of assorted vegetables interspersed with pineapples cut into the shape of flowers. The platter was white with delicate paintings of even more fricken flowers. "Sure," I replied, grabbing a piece of celery and dipping it in ranch sauce.

"What's with Melissa?" Adonis asked around a mouthful of a pig in a blanket.

I leaned against the front door—it was the only patch of unoccupied wall left—and took a bite of my celery, enjoying the crunch almost as much as making Adonis wait for an answer. "We've been gone for over twenty-four hours, and her mom didn't notice."

"Oh." Adonis' voice went solemn in understanding.

I wished I understood. Big deal if Melissa's mom didn't notice she was gone. Wasn't *not* getting into trouble a good thing? But Melissa had sounded happy at the prospect of getting "killed" by her mother. Like doing something as extreme as flying to another city, stealing a car, and vanishing with no word of where she'd gone would force Minthe to notice her.

Weird, I didn't think humans needed worship to survive like we did. But maybe teenagers were different.

"Who are you?" A gray-eyed goddess asked.

I blinked, jolted from my reverie. "Aphrodite."

"You're new," she observed. She didn't introduce herself. "I'll let you guess."

I nodded, taking in her studious look. Charisma radiated off her in waves, subtle, but powerful and well controlled. I ticked off the short mental list of Zeus' known daughters. "Athena?"

The name clicked into place, sending an onslaught of images and information through my head. Goddess of wisdom, liked horses, tended toward neutrality but never quite managed it. Thousands of details flickered to life in an instant. Knowing everything kind of hurt sometimes.

Still, it was better than a cold introduction. By allowing me to guess, she'd given me the chance to pull up most of the information on my own, so recovering from the knowledge dump wasn't as brutal as it could have been.

"Good guess."

"Nice to meet you," I said with a grimace.

Athena gave me an understanding smile. "And you are?" She motioned to Adonis.

A flare of jealousy flashed through me, but I dismissed it. Adonis' opinion of me came across crystal clear on the trip home. Rejection didn't come easy for me, but I wasn't about to get worked up over some lowly demigod.

"Wouldn't you like to know?" Adonis said with a grin.

Irritation flickered across Athena's face, and I smiled, happy to know I wasn't the only one who didn't like him. Melissa had hung on his every word all afternoon. It was annoying.

Athena saw my look and gave me a warm smile in return. My grin broadened. I felt a sense of kinship with her because she didn't seem to wish I'd never been born. That pretty much made her the nicest person I'd ever met.

The doorbell rang, and since no one else moved to get it, I turned and pulled the door open. A man wearing a black leather jacket stood on the porch.

Not just any man. Tall. Dark. Handsome. And a god. Nice. I stood speechless, captivated by his fiery eyes. He seemed equally stunned and let out a low whistle.

"Got to say," he murmured in a voice almost too low to hear. "I'm liking the newer models."

"And just who the hell are you?"

He shot me a rakish grin. "Ares."

God of war. Bloodshed, screams, battle cries. People dying by the thousands. A wooden horse. Fire. Blackened bodies. Sick and wounded soldiers with melting faces. The images came too fast. Too overwhelming. I tore my gaze away from him and stepped back, stumbling in my haste. He stepped forward and grabbed my arm, steadying me.

"That was stupid of me, I'm sorry." He sounded like he meant it. "It's been a long time since I've met a new deity. I should have let you guess."

"Everything all right here?" Adonis' voice came from somewhere over my left shoulder.

"And if it wasn't? What would you do about it, half breed?" When Adonis didn't reply, Ares smirked. "Yeah, I thought so."

He moved past me and stalked into the room. Everyone fell silent. I stood, staring at the open door, too stunned to turn and investigate the silence behind me. All those dying people . . .

Adonis moved between me and the door, breaking my gaze. He studied my face. "Hey, what happened?"

Behind me, Ares and Athena started arguing. I couldn't focus on the words. I just kept seeing the bodies, the blood, and the death.

"Aphrodite?"

I shook my head to clear it. What was I doing standing here in shock over the death of a few . . . million . . . humans? Humans died, it happened. War was great for gods. There's no beating wartime worship. Fear and desperation gave it a potency that was hard to replicate in the day to day goings on of the typical human life.

But their faces . . .

"Aphrodite?" Adonis touched my shoulder. "Are you okay?"

I pulled away from him, temper flaring. "What do you care?"

Spinning on my heel, I stalked off. Stupid humans and their stupid wars and their stupid lies and fake concern. And stupid me, for giving a damn about any of them.

Chapter XVII

Hades

"ARE YOU SURE this is the right place?" I stared at the . . . I could only describe it as a church, half hoping Demeter had the wrong address. Only half. It had taken Demeter weeks to track down Apollo. We'd found almost everyone else.

Persephone hadn't turned up in the Underworld, which meant she was still alive. Zeus had to be hurting her so badly that it took all the power she had to heal, so her excess power didn't kill her.

That was sort of good news. Gods, I hated Zeus. Only he could turn the world upside down enough for me to see a bright side to my wife being tortured.

Demeter motioned to the sign on the church. "Unfortunately."

It *looked* like a church, which was odd in itself in this industrial area, but instead of crosses and such on the stained glass windows there were suns everywhere.

Staring at the billboard that proclaimed, "WE WORSHIP THE SUN" in disbelief, I couldn't decide if I was horrified or impressed. Silhouettes of bikini-clad girls in sunglasses lined either side of the sign. Unbelievable. Apollo had started a cult in the center of L.A, a large city by human standards, while the rest of the gods were hidden in the shadows struggling to find enough worship to survive. And no one noticed.

Apollo had always been a bit eccentric, but this?

"Wazzup!" A group of kids in board shorts approached a gaggle of girls in daisy dukes and bikini tops.

Wazzup," they replied in solemn voices.

The two groups bowed to each other, and I thought I might have an apoplexy.

Demeter took a deep breath and walked in the door. I followed, pushing aside the beaded curtains to find myself in a stripped-down sanctuary that smelled sickly sweet.

"Wazzup!" a group of very tan people called to us.

I looked to Demeter, letting her take the lead. This was still her realm.

"Quite a bit," Demeter replied. "We were wondering if we could speak with. . . ." She hesitated like she couldn't bring herself to say it. ". . . Mr. Sunshine, please."

Really? I thought, unable to suppress a groan. Oh, Apollo was *never* going to live this down.

The group of kids exchanged a glance. "He doesn't usually talk to old folks, man. Sorry."

Demeter's mouth dropped open. "Old . . . people. Uh . . . I see."

I didn't. Physically, all the gods stopped aging at the end of maturity, so we didn't look older than twenty-five unless we wanted to. How were we considered old compared to him? I looked down at the deep maroon carpet flecked with pieces of grass and sighed. Good gods. I missed the Underworld.

"Why don't you tell him his Aunt Ceres is here and see what he says," Demeter suggested.

"Yo, Mr. Sunshine!" one of the youths called, running down the hall to an office with yet another beaded curtain. "Your Great-Aunt Sarah is here."

A vein in Demeter's forehead twitched, and I smiled despite myself. It was nice to see Demeter knocked off her pedestal. Even by these creatures.

Apollo tore out of the office so fast he got tangled in the beaded curtain and ripped it down in his haste to get free. My eyes narrowed when I took him in. His matted red hair was cut short, he had a scruff of a beard beginning on his face, and he wore clothes with holes and patches on them.

"Why does he look homeless?" I murmured.

Demeter shook her head. "Not homeless, ironic."

Oh good gods.

"Demeter!" Apollo managed to get mostly untangled from the curtain and moved forward in jerky motions while he tried to shake it off his foot.

"I let you live in my realm after the fall, and *this* is how you repay me?" Demeter's eyes blazed. She looked around, like she was considering moving to a more quiet location, then dismissed Apollo's inebriated followers with a snort. "You started your own cult."

"I meant to send tribute, throw your name in services every now and then, I just get so . . . distracted."

As if to underscore his point, a half-naked girl peeked her head out the office door. "Mr. Sunshine? Are you coming back?"

"Uh . . . not right now."

A chorus of disappointed wails rose from the office, and my eyebrows shot up.

Apollo's face turned beet red and he closed his eyes, took a deep breath, then cracked one eye open as if hoping we wouldn't be there.

"I see." Demeter's voice was like ice. "You think you can poach my followers."

"There are seven billion people on this planet. You can't have them all!" Apollo protested. Demeter compressed her lips into a thin white line, and he stammered an apology. When he noticed me, his face drained of color. "Aw shit, Demeter. There was no reason to get him involved. I'll mention your name every harvest, I promise. I've got some girls—erm . . . priestesses, I mean, I can send your way. Don't make me go to the Underworld."

"Harvest?" Demeter demanded. "What harvest?"

I held up my hands in a placating gesture. "No, you're welcome to live forever as far as I'm concerned. No need to come to my realm. Ever."

"How many priestesses do you want?" Apollo asked Demeter. "Hey girls?" He called a little louder.

"Yes, Mr. Sunshine?" The girls emerged from the office in various stages of undress.

"Oh please, don't bother." Demeter had a look on her face like she'd like to remove her eyes and scour them with bleach. "There's more important things going on right now, and as it just so happens, you owe me."

Demeter explained what was going on with Zeus, and Apollo turned even paler.

"Uh, yeah, that sucks about your kid and all, but that isn't really my scene. I'm a lover not a fighter, and uh—"

Demeter walked up to him until they were standing nose to nose. "Do you like living in my realm?"

Apollo nodded.

"Do you want to continue?"

He nodded again.

"Then you'd best come with us." When Apollo nodded again, Demeter wrinkled her nose and touched her fingertips to him, establishing the bare minimum of contact to teleport. She reached behind her to grab my hand, and we disappeared in a flash.

When I opened my eyes, we were standing in the middle of Demeter's crowded living room. Two raised voices caught my attention. I turned to see Ares and Athena arguing with one another.

"Go shower," Demeter told Apollo. "Then we'll talk."

Apollo took a quick look around at the assembled mass of gods, then stumbled back and bolted up the stairs.

"Oh sure, Demeter." Sarcasm laced my voice. "A shower's going to fix everything."

A hint of a smile twitched on Demeter's face. "I don't see why you're so worried Hades. With *Mr. Sunshine* on our side, how can we lose?"

I laughed despite myself, and Demeter's composure broke into snorting giggles. Everyone stopped talking to stare at us, but I didn't care. Not about them anyway.

A wave of pain washed through me, cutting my laughter short. Persephone was in pain again.

Chapter XVIII

Persephone

"WHAT A WASTE," Hades sneered.

Whatever. At least he wasn't making out with Aphrodite anymore. Or Melissa.

Or my mom. That had been disturbing on a whole new level. I think I preferred being struck by lightning.

"Has anyone ever told you that you are way too interested in Hades' love life?" I asked, interrupting speech number one thousand nine hundred eighty-one on how useless, worthless, and otherwise awful I was.

Of course, anything was preferable to watching Zeus rip them apart limb by limb. I think even he realized he'd gone too far with that set of dreams. He'd given me almost a week to recuperate.

I still saw them writhing with agony when I closed my eyes. Still heard them screaming for me to save them. Cursing me for causing their pain.

He'd been wearing my face that time.

"It's kind of pathetic." I yawned. "Did you ever even like Hera, or did you just like that he liked her?"

"You're nothing compared to Hera." Hades' face twisted into a malicious grin. "She was—"

"Amazing, spectacular, beautiful, perfect." I ticked off the meaningless attributes on my fingers. "Yeah, I got the memo. She was also crazy to have picked *you* over him. But whatever. I owe her one. Why do *you* care so much? Jealous of your big brother, or does this go deeper?"

He shifted back into Zeus. "I have nothing to be jealous of."

"People like him of their own volition," I pointed out. "Love him even. He doesn't have to resort to charm. Much less torture."

Zeus narrowed his eyes at me. "You think so? Maybe I should tell you about some of the things he's done. Better yet—" a curved blade appeared in his hand "—how about I just show you?"

Chapter XIX

Aphrodite

SLIPPING AWAY from Melissa long enough to dreamwalk wasn't easy. As much as she complained, she took her job as my babysitter seriously, never letting me out of her sight for more than a few seconds.

But Melissa had been recruited for cleanup duty, so I slipped away and locked myself in the bedroom, lay on the bed, and closed my eyes. Dreamwalking was easy, like taking a deep breath and going under water. It didn't take me long to find Persephone.

When I found her mind wide open, I paused, tempted to go get Hades. He and Demeter had been taking shifts, trying to dreamwalk to Persephone for weeks, but she never seemed to be asleep. Either that or she was so far from consciousness that she couldn't open her mind to visitors.

No. If I took the time to warn Hades, she might not be here when I came back. Zeus wouldn't let her stay under for more than a few minutes. I closed my eyes and stepped into her dream.

Persephone sat against a transparent wall that looked out over a bright blue sky. Her knees were drawn up to her chest, her head ducked down, and her hands clasped over her ears.

I touched her shoulder, and she jolted forward with a surprised cry. Her tear-streaked face turned to me. She blinked as her green eyes focused.

"Okay . . ." she said after a moment. "This is weird even for you."

"Are you okay?" Dumb question. She'd been curled up in the fetal position, spending her sleeping hours in tears.

"What do you care?" She climbed to her feet and swept a tangle of wavy blond hair off her shoulders. "So what are you going to do next? Annoy me to death?"

"What?" I drew my eyebrows together in confusion. "Look, we don't have much time. I don't know how much longer Zeus is going to let you sleep. Where are you?"

She snorted and sank back to the ground, drawing her knees up to her chest beneath her long white dress. The dress covered her feet, pooling onto the floor around her. Persephone crossed her arms over her knees and ducked her head, sending her hair cascading down her shoulders and over her arms. I bit my lip, recognizing a shield when I saw one. Not a real shield—she wasn't using power. Pressed up to the wall behind her, Persephone vanished into herself as a shapeless blob of fabric and hair. "Go away."

"Look—" I knelt beside her. "I get you're mad at me. I didn't want to help Zeus, but I didn't have a choice. It's a long story, and Hades can explain it better than I can anyway. Hades and I . . ." I trailed off, trying to get my thoughts together. She was acting so weird it was hard to stop babbling and get to a point, but I couldn't have much time left.

"Right, she and Hades. He's never given her a second look, so you can stop *that* train of thought right there." Her voice was muffled as she spoke into her skirt. She wouldn't look at me.

"Um. No. Hades is like, ancient." He was also off-the-charts hot, even for a god. I'd be lying if I said I hadn't given it a thought, but he and Persephone seemed to be going for the whole monogamy thing, and I respected her way too much to steal her guy.

Still, he'd give me way more than a second look if I wanted him to. But she didn't need to hear that right now.

Wait a minute! Persephone said "she," like I wasn't me. "You think I'm Zeus. I'm not. I'm Aphrodite, no tricks, no deception. Hades and your mom and pretty much every other god on the planet are looking for you. So I'm going to ask one more time. Where are you?"

She raised her head, green eyes searching my face. "Aphrodite?" She let out a long breath. "Is this real? Sometimes I . . . I see things that aren't . . ." She trailed off, looking small and frail.

"I'm real," I assured her.

"I'm in his realm, in a castle in the sky." She looked around like she could find something else to help me find her, but all that surrounded her were windows looking out to endless sky. "It was daylight when I passed out. You?"

I nodded. "Daylight, so you're in the same hemisphere."

"Glad to help narrow it down." Her voice was bitter.

"It's more than we knew ten minutes ago."

"What happened to Hades?" She sounded so scared I did a double take. "I can't hear him. Is he . . . ?"

"He's fine. Going nuts trying to find you, but that's what I'm here about." I took a deep breath. "He's hoping to convince one of Zeus' other kids to kill off Zeus—"

"But failing that, I need to do it." She sighed. "Aphrodite, I'm not strong enough. I've been fighting *back*. I just—"

"I know. And Hades doesn't want you to get your hands dirty. His plan is stupid, Persephone. And dangerous."

She gave me an expectant look, so I continued.

"He wants to reset the rules. Make it easier to kill gods."

"He can do that?"

I snorted. "Persephone, he helped create the world. As long as he can get enough of the original six on board, he can do anything. But there's a price. A balance. And if he screws it up, all of creation could be forfeit."

"He won't do it then."

"I think you underestimate his devotion to you."

She shook her head. "He has a life outside of me with people who matter. He won't risk them for me anymore than I would risk my people for him. He's panicked, and worried, but I don't believe he'll risk all of creation to find me."

"Okay." She hadn't seen his face when he said he was going to kill Zeus. "But last resort, Persephone, I need you to promise you won't let him."

She tilted her head to the side. "And I'm supposed to stop him . . . how exactly?"

I took a deep breath, wishing I could stand. It was getting uncomfortable crouching down like this. But Persephone was just starting to sound like herself again, and I didn't want to risk any sudden movements. "If it looks like nothing else will work, and you can't kill Zeus—"

"It's not like I haven't been fighting back! If I could kill him—"

"Yeah, yeah, whatever." I waved a dismissive hand. "If there's nothing else to try, then you need to take yourself out of the equation."

She blinked, processing that. Her eyebrows drew together like she was turning my words over in her mind to make sense of them. Understanding dawned in her expression. Her mouth dropped open. *"That's your plan? You want me to die?"*

"No! Like I said, last resort."

"Absolutely not!" She sprang to her feet, glowering at me. "Are you sure you're not Zeus?"

"I'm not Zeus." I stood, slow, holding my hands up in a placating gesture.

"Then are you working for him? Because seriously, Aphrodite, this is screwed up even for you."

I tossed my hair back and rolled my eyes. "Look, there is no threat if you don't exist. I don't know why you're so offended. I said last resort, and self-sacrifice is kind of your MO."

"What are you talking about?" The sun sparkled in through the window, bathing Persephone in bright light. It glistened off her skin and hair, making her look like some kind of avenging angel.

"Boreas, Thanatos, Zeus. You shouldn't have gone up against any of them because you had no hope of winning. Just because I thought of it first doesn't make it any less noble or whatever. Bonus, you'd be saving all the realms, not just your annoying friend."

"Get out." Her fists, clenched to her side, didn't hide the fact she was shaking with indignation.

"Persephone—"

"Get *out*, Aphrodite!"

I sighed. "Are you aware that I *have* to obey direct commands from you or anyone else in Zeus' bloodline who outranks me?"

She blinked. "No, I thought it was just Zeus. Fine." She gritted her teeth and took a deep breath. "Please, get the hell out!"

"I'll leave. But take this." I shoved a small pearl at her. "If you change your mind just break it, and I'll put you out of your misery. Don't worry," I said, cutting off her objections. "It won't break unless you want it to. I'll know."

She ignored my outstretched hand, and I let out an impatient huff. "Look, sometimes death can be a mercy. I don't want you to die. And I really hope you're right about Hades, but he's not thinking clearly—"

"And you think me committing suicide will make him more rational?" She rolled her eyes to show how little she thought of that idea.

"No, it will drive him nuts. But he's not going to risk the world if there's no saving you. Plus—" I fell silent long enough to make sure I had her full attention "—if Hades makes it easier to kill gods, who do you think the rest of the gods are going to come for first?"

I let her chew on that for a minute, then grabbed her hand and pressed the pearl into it. "Don't let it come to this."

"Aphrodite . . ." Persephone didn't look angry anymore, she looked small and frightened. "If I take that, I'll use it."

"No." I put a hand on her shoulder. "You'll wait until there's absolutely no other chance left. You're strong. You never stop fighting."

Her green eyes locked with mine, and I was startled at the glint of iron in them. She might believe she was broken, but Persephone was far stronger than she knew.

"Aphrodite, I won't stop you from swearing over to me and throwing all your power my way, putting an end to this miserable existence. But I sure as hell don't have to help you justify it. Don't come here asking me to be all strong and noble when in reality you're just too weak to make the decision yourself. I've made *enough* hard choices."

"Persephone—"

"No! I'm telling you that if you give me that thing I. Will. Use. It. When he's hurting me, all I can think of is making the pain stop. I'm in no position to judge when we've reached the 'last resort,'" she put the words in air quotes, "so don't delude yourself into thinking you're washing your hands of this by making me pull the trigger. If you give me that, *you're the one killing me.*"

Shame filled me when I realized she was right. Knowing what I needed to do should it come to it was one thing, but I didn't want to be the one to do it. All this time I'd been so furious all my choices had been taken from me, and here I was trying to force a kill order out of Persephone so I didn't have to make the decision. Still, I was glad I'd told her. She didn't think Hades was going to take the risk, but she hadn't expressly forbade me from pulling her plug either. I knew what she wanted should Hades go completely off the rails. Maybe that would make it easier.

Somehow I doubted it. "I'm sorry. Persephone, I'm so sorry you're here right now, and for my part in all this, and—"

She hugged me. "You didn't have a choice. I'm sorry I ever suspected you were Zeus."

Suddenly, I felt a pulling sensation and was ripped away from the dream.

Zeus had woken her up.

I bolted upright with a gasp and found myself facing an angry-looking Melissa.

Though let's face it. It's not like she ever looked happy.

"What were you doing?" she demanded.

I frowned. "Taking a nap."

"The whole truth. Tell me everything." Her steely gaze made it clear I wasn't leaving this room until I complied.

So I did.

Chapter XX

Hades

"THERE?" I POINTED to a spot on the map in the middle of no-wheresville Alabama. "You're sure?"

"As sure as I can be," Apollo replied. "She moves around a lot." He drummed his fingers against Demeter's teak dining room table. "You really think she'll be any help?"

More than you. I smirked, but didn't allow the thought to pass through my lips.

A knock on the half-open door brought my head up. Melissa peeked into the dining room. "Can I speak with you?" She gave Apollo a pointed look. "Alone."

Raising an eyebrow, Apollo shot me a questioning look. I inclined my head, granting him permission to leave the room. When he passed Melissa, he turned back, eyes roaming over her in an appreciative once-over.

I caught his eye with my best *over my dead body* look. Persephone wouldn't thank me if I let Apollo take advantage of her best friend.

Melissa shut the door on Apollo's face, hard. "Can you shield us?"

Intrigued, I nodded and dropped a shield around the room so we couldn't be overheard. "Something wrong?"

"Aphrodite told me what you have planned."

I sighed and shoved my hair out of my face. "Of course she did. Look, Melissa. I appreciate your concern, but—"

"Don't talk down to me. I'm every bit as old as your wife and a great deal smarter. Aphrodite said if you screwed up you'd be risking every-thing. Everyone. Is that true?"

Well . . . that was to the point. "I don't intend to mess up."

"You can promise you won't?"

I opened my mouth. Closed it. No, I couldn't. There was always a risk.

Her dark eyes locked to mine. "Yeah, I thought so. Why not give

Aphrodite's plan a shot? Have Persephone kill Zeus."

"She's not strong enough."

Melissa snorted. "Yeah, you've known her for like five minutes. I've known her my whole life. She'll kill him if she has to. If for no other reason than to keep *us* safe. She doesn't like confrontation, but she's pretty hardcore if she gets caught in a corner."

"I know," I assured her. "Persephone's stronger than she thinks. But she doesn't have enough power to defeat Zeus. And if we follow Aphrodite's plan and convince everyone to swear over to her, she'll die."

Melissa chewed on her bottom lip. "She can get out of this. And she doesn't need anyone else's powers to do it."

It was obvious by the troubled look in her eyes that she didn't believe herself, but I wasn't going to shatter whatever lies she told herself to sleep at night. "It's good you have so much faith in her."

Melissa shrugged. "It's my job. Look, Hades, I love Persephone. And I love you for caring enough to risk everything to save her. Seriously. But she wouldn't want you to do this, and you know it."

I pulled out a chair and motioned for her to sit down. "Did you know Zeus' realm used to be populated?"

She shook her head. I sat across from her and looked her straight in the eye. "Sentient creatures. As large a population as there ever was in this realm or Poseidon's."

"What happened to them?"

"Zeus. You don't want him to win this, Melissa. He uses people up and then they die. I have entire sub-realms in the Underworld full of his victims. They deserve better than to be at his mercy again, and so does everyone in your realm. As much as I love Persephone, this isn't just about her. It's about every living being in creation. I can't let Zeus happen to them."

She swallowed hard and nodded. "I appreciate that. But as one of those living beings you're protecting, can I give you some feedback?"

I smiled, amused. "Why not?"

"You're overstepping. We don't need you to protect us from Zeus. We don't *need* you at all. If Zeus thinks he can take down the human race, he's going to have another thing coming."

Chapter XXI

Hades

I WAS STILL MULLING over my conversation with Melissa when I left Demeter's to track down Artemis. Demeter had finally granted me teleportation rights. Far too late to help Persephone, of course, but it could come in handy in the future.

A twig snapped beneath my foot. Swearing, I slapped at a mosquito. I didn't care for forests, but this was where Artemis spent most of her time during hunting season. Apollo said she had a cabin out here . . . somewhere. I just needed to find it.

Another twig snapped. I frowned at my feet, but didn't see any broken branches.

Something cold touched the base of my neck.

"Don't move," a gruff voice instructed.

I turned with a sigh, grabbing the gun out of the hunter's hand before he could fire off a shot. Not that it would have hurt me more than that mosquito bite, but it could be damned uncomfortable, which made it at least as annoying.

The gun crumbled to dust in my hand, and I gave the stranger my least friendly smile. The blood drained from his face. Before I could comment on his predicament, a cry rang through the clearing.

"Diana!" The hunter spun on his heel and tore through the forest.

Diana? When Artemis' pseudonym clicked, I swore and followed him, casting a shield as far ahead of us as I could see so our progress through the forest couldn't be seen or heard. Before we reached a small clearing with a cabin, I threw a second shield at the hunter, freezing him in place.

I walked to the edge of the clearing. Beyond the shield, Zeus held a struggling woman just above his head by the throat. She pried at his fingers with both hands, legs kicking uselessly at the ground but finding no purchase.

"I can make this easy for you, or I can make it fun for me." A grin spread across Zeus' face. "Swear fealty now, and your death will be less interesting, but infinitely less painful."

"No," she gasped. Her body stiffened, muscles going rigid, and the smell of burnt flesh and ozone wafted through the clearing. Behind me, the hunter yelled, straining against the shield. Maybe I could sneak up behind Zeus and . . . no, shit, if he teleported with her, all bets were off. I closed my eyes, concentrating, and crafted a shield just above his head that took in the whole clearing, then dropped the shield between Zeus and myself out of necessity, but kept the one around the hunter. The last thing I needed to do was give Zeus more leverage.

Zeus started. "Hades. What a nice surprise."

He lowered Artemis to the ground, spinning her to face me, looping his left arm around her neck, and gripping his right bicep. His right hand shoved her head forward. Grinning, he brought his elbows together in a tight chokehold. Sweat glistened against her caramel skin, plastering the dark wisps of hair that had escaped her ponytail to her face. *Get me out of this*, her eyes seemed to beg. *I'll owe you.*

Shit.

"You've got ten seconds." Zeus gave me an expectant look. "When she drops, I'm gone."

I inclined my head to the shield around him. "Unlikely."

Zeus' face twisted in a scowl. "We'll see. Are you here to surrender your realm?"

"No." My mind raced to find a way to trap him without Artemis getting caught in the crossfire. I could create an entrance to the Underworld and pull enough of my realm through to trap him in the same type of prison that held the Titans, but she'd be stuck with him.

It might be worth it.

"Then we have nothing to discuss." Zeus tightened his grip around Artemis' throat, and she slumped in his arms. "Except, I've been meaning to get this to you." He took advantage of Artemis' lapse in consciousness long enough to reach in his pocket and toss something to me across the clearing in a blur of pink. Artemis regained consciousness, sputtering for breath. She lurched forward, but he had her back in the chokehold in seconds.

I caught Persephone's phone out of reflex. It took me a second to place the picture of the mangled mass of flesh on the screen as something humanoid, much less recognize it as my wife. My stomach lurched.

"There's some great videos on there too," Zeus informed me. "In case you need some incentive to change your mind." As if on cue,

Persephone's screams burst from the phone's tiny speakers.

I yanked on the power of the Underworld, ripping it through the earth in my rage. Artemis' eyes widened as she realized what I was doing. "I swear fealty!" she cried as the ground split beneath her. Her dark eyes met mine, and before I could say anything to stop her she added, "To Hades."

Her power flashed through me, knocking me off balance just long enough for the shield above Zeus to flicker. He growled and threw her to the ground.

"No!" I shouted as Zeus leapt into the air and vanished.

Artemis stood and faced me, movements slow and deliberate. "You were going to *trap* me with him?"

I pocketed Persephone's phone and dropped the shield around Artemis' boyfriend.

Artemis' gaze didn't even flicker in his direction. "Answer me!"

"You wouldn't like what I have to say."

"Diana!" The hunter ran to her, but she held out a hand, keeping him at arm's length.

"I wouldn't like what you have to say? You were going to trap me in Tartarus with that sadistic son of a bitch, and all you can say for yourself is that I wouldn't like what you have to say!" Her dark eyes blazed with fury. "What the hell is wrong with you, Hades? We go back, way back. I thought we were friends, but you were willing to abandon me, for what, some slip of a girl you just met?" She held her chin up, using every inch of her five feet to try to make me feel small, but I wasn't having it.

"You could have teleported!" I threw my hands in the air. "You could have escaped before he so much as touched you. What the hell were you still doing here?" Her gaze flickered to the hunter then back to me, the movement almost imperceptible and probably unintentional. I let out a dark laugh. "Protecting your latest human pet? I kept him out of the line of fire for you, but since you were so determined to swear away your sanity, I sure as hell wasn't going to put my wife on the line to stop you. Here—" I stepped forward, grabbing her shoulder and shoving her powers back into her before breaking the bond of fealty with a snap.

She stumbled and suddenly a hand yanked on my shoulder. "Don't touch her!" The hunter shouted, fist flying toward my face.

I caught it in a bone-crunching grip.

"Stop!" Artemis darted between us. "Oh, Ryan—" She took his hand, and I felt a pinprick of power flow between them as she healed him. He stared at her, wide-eyed. "What the hell is going on?"

"It's a long story." Her shoulders slumped, and she returned her attention to me. "He comes with us."

"Like hell!"

"I'm not stupid, Hades. Zeus has your wife, and you want him dead. I'm one of the few people who can make that happen." She tilted her chin up, eyes glittering with defiance. "If you want my help. He comes too."

Chapter XXII

Persephone

"I'M IMPRESSED." Zeus still looked like Hades as he stroked my cheek. "I didn't expect you to hold out this long."

Thinking of the pearl Aphrodite offered me, I realized she'd been right all along.

Death could be a mercy. The torture blended together in such a painful haze that I'd lost the ability to distinguish between the waking world and dreamscapes. Propped up against that familiar wall of mist, my hand clutched my necklace. I was crushing the poor plant, but I couldn't seem to loosen my grip.

I'd been prepared for pain when Zeus stormed into the room, but he seemed even more agitated than usual. And he'd taken it out on me.

Gods, I was in so much pain. It was probably a dream. If he wasn't electrocuting me anymore, I was most likely dreaming.

"The question is how are you still refusing me? You're not this strong."

Sometimes he looked like Hades when I was awake though. It was hard to tell. Was I awake, or was I sleeping?

Did it matter?

He was still talking. As he launched into his insulting tirade, I smiled to myself. Zeus was losing ground. The list of insults grew shorter by the day. He could no longer call me weak because of what I'd survived, he couldn't call me common because he couldn't figure me out, and he'd even lost stupid because he knew I would have broken by now if I hadn't found some way around swearing fealty.

Sure, he could still say hurtful things. Terrible things if I allowed myself to focus on them. But the shock of hearing insults from Hades' voice had long since worn off. Besides, I was in high school. I'd heard way worse.

I couldn't allow myself to look too comfortable. When Zeus saw something wasn't working, he found some new hell to put me through.

Each of his ideas was worse than the last.

Was I dreaming? I'd figured out how to tell once, but I'd forgotten when I came to. It was something important. Something I might be able to do next time I was under.

Zeus' face rippled, twisting back to his own features. "They're building an army down on the surface. Just to find you. Every remaining god under one roof, driven together for a common purpose." He grinned, like that made him happy for some reason. "What makes you so special?" He looked at me like he wanted to slice me open and see what made me tick. "What does he see in you?"

There was a way to tell. The memory slid around my brain like water, but I couldn't grab hold of a thought long enough to think it. He'd broken my mind, shattered it into a thousand pieces. Meh, who needed recall abilities? *Something* in my mind was whole and present, otherwise I wouldn't still be walking and talking. The longer I sat here, the more it healed. "Their common purpose isn't me. It's you. Everyone hates you enough to want you dead. Can you blame them?"

"I was their hero once." He almost sounded sad.

I snorted and rolled my eyes, letting my head loll against the wall of mist. This was as close to rest as I got. I was going to take advantage of it. "And now you're psychotic." I shrugged. "It happens."

His eyes narrowed. "Your mother didn't seem to mind."

Oh, he had *not* just gone there. "I've never had to ask what her biggest regret was."

"You?"

I laughed. "Hardly. She loves me more than *anything*. But I guess you wouldn't know what that's like. Your parents thought you were an abomination—"

"Shut up."

In a flash, I remembered. Most of my powers didn't work in his realm, but I could set the rules in my own head. "My mom hates you, you know. But I guess that shouldn't surprise you. I can't think of a single person or deity who doesn't." When I was sure his attention was fully on me, I concentrated on using my powers. A small red poppy grew in the corner of the room behind Zeus.

A dream. Perfect. Fractured pieces of the plan I'd put together during the rare times I was conscious enough to think came to me. I drew in a deep breath. I'd never tried anything like this before, so there was a big chance my plan wouldn't work. But at this point I'd take any chance, no matter how slim. "You *created* Aphrodite to be loyal to you, and even she can't stand you."

Rage reddened his face. "You're going to want to be very careful what you say to me."

I concentrated hard enough to make vines shoot around his legs, holding him in place.

"You're in my head, remember." I was probably going to regret this when I came to. But really, he already tortured me all day. What did I have to lose? Stepping outside of my dream, I called "*Adios.*"

My mind closed to all visitors, locking down my dreamscape without me in it. I didn't know how that worked or how soon Zeus would be able to get out, but if I could keep Zeus occupied even for a few minutes . . .

My eyes shot open, and I sprang out of bed. Throwing open the door to the bedroom, I looked up and down the misty hallway. Which way led to the exit?

Turning right, I sprinted down the hall until I came to a huge room filled with sunlight and a massive door of mist. I pulled it open and gaped at the endless sky that spread in all directions. If there was land beneath me, I couldn't see it. I swallowed hard. This was probably going to hurt.

Chapter XXIII

Aphrodite

I YAWNED AND inspected my nails. Divine meetings were boring as hell.

Hades stood in the front of the room, his dark clothes sucking in the cheery brightness of Demeter's home like a black hole. "Who are we missing?" Hades paused, deep in thought, gaze fixed on Demeter's white couch. "Is anyone else still around?"

"Hebe?" Ares suggested. He hadn't shed the jacket, despite the stifling heat of the overcrowded home.

I winced, expecting an onslaught of information and images to rush over me, but there wasn't much to know about Hebe. She was the goddess of youth, and apparently—

"Dead," Hades confirmed.

I would have thought a goddess of youth would be safe. This culture seemed to worship it enough.

"Eileithyia?" one of the muses asked, referring to the goddess of the pain of childbirth.

Wait, seriously? I racked my brain and came up with hundreds upon thousands of useless gods of mists and doorways and clouds. No wonder so many of the gods were dead. What a waste of worship.

"She didn't last very long after they invented the epidural." Demeter sat on her couch, feet tucked under her, drinking a cup of steaming tea. If having so many deities running freely through her home bothered her, she didn't show it.

The humans on the other hand looked ready to crawl out of their skin. With the exception of the new human, Ryan, they sat clustered at the kitchen table as though they were clinging to safety in numbers as a defense against the massive gathering of gods. Ryan was still upstairs with Artemis getting filled in on all things divine. Lucky him. Adonis, Melissa, Orpheus, and Eurydice looked like they'd rather be *anywhere* else, including Tartarus.

"Hephaestus?" Apollo hopped off the last step of the staircase, rubbing his wet hair with a towel. He looked almost normal in blue jeans and a white T-shirt with a smiling sun wearing sunglasses.

Everyone in the room fell silent. At first I thought they were snubbing Apollo, then the name he'd said hit my system.

The information came so fast that it almost didn't have time to process. Raised voices, a stack of weapons glittering in the sun, a flash of lightning, and a cry of pain, discord on Olympus followed by averted eyes and buried guilt. Wow! There was some history there.

"Let's . . . not involve him," Demeter suggested. The tension in the room eased palpably.

Not involve him? We needed all the help we could get.

I looked across the room at Melissa, and she inclined her head in a slight nod. Smiling, I found myself glad she was on board with my unspoken plan to recruit Hephaestus. Melissa wasn't so bad. At least not when she acted more like me and less like an entitled selfish brat. I was pleased to be rubbing off on her. It's not often one can claim credit for making the world a less irritating place, but I wasn't going to let the accomplishment go to my head.

Persephone deserved the best possible chance. The best way of giving her that was to bring as many gods into this as possible. However uncomfortable the rest of the gods were with what had happened, no one could deny Hephaestus was powerful.

Demeter seemed to notice Adonis for the first time. "Who is that?" She leaned forward, placing her tea on a wicker side table and fixed Adonis with a penetrating glare.

Melissa smirked. "Aphrodite and I found him. He's Zeus'. We figured he'd be next on the hit list—"

"And what?" Demeter demanded. "You felt we had the extra resources to protect him right now?"

Melissa seemed surprised, but I understood what Demeter was getting at. We didn't have the manpower to keep our eyes on another person. I had pretty much taken up all the leeway left. But I had a solution. "I thought he could stay in the Underworld."

"Wait, what?" This was news to Adonis.

I nodded. The Underworld was safe. Though whether I thought it kept Adonis safe, or us safe from Adonis, I wasn't sure. Something about him gave me the creeps. "Hades, don't you need a few extra hands down there anyway? I just thought—"

"I'm not going to the Underworld!" Adonis objected.

Orpheus hushed him, and the rest of the gods seemed to decide it was time to explore the house.

Demeter ignored Adonis, her eyes focused on me, glittering with rage. "We can't trust you for help or ideas, and you know that. Anything you say is automatically suspect—"

"Why?" Adonis asked.

"Shut up!" Orpheus hissed. He grabbed the young demigod's arm and made as if to lead him from the room, but drew up short when Hades stepped in from of him.

Hades' electric-blue eyes swept over Adonis with such intensity Adonis seemed to shrink in on himself. "There's something different about this one," Hades murmured.

Orpheus gave Adonis an apologetic look, felt backward for Eurydice's hand, and retreated from the room, pulling her along with him. Smart man.

"He's one of Zeus' eugenics projects." Demeter waved a dismissive hand. "That's why I hadn't bothered with him. Zeus isn't likely to come after—"

"Eugenics?" Hades' eyebrows shot up.

Demeter either missed or just didn't care about the warning in his tone. "His mother was a demigod, so was his grandmother, and her mother before that, and her mother before that going back centuries. His father had the same type of—"

"His father?" I leaned forward. "His father is Zeus. He's got charm. I can feel it."

"No." Demeter clasped her hands together. "His grandfather is Zeus, on both sides, and his great-grandfather and his great-great grandfather." The list continued for a few more generations, but we got the gist of it. Adonis was inbred to the extreme.

Adonis sat down in the chair fast. He looked ill.

"Zeus isn't going to kill him," Demeter continued. "I'm sure there's a female version of him out there somewhere he'll be compelled to breed with. Zeus will be curious to see what happens with their child."

"He has charm," I repeated, unable to believe *anyone* not directly descended from a god could have powers. Demigods didn't pass on powers to their children. They didn't even pass on ichor, the golden blood of the gods that gave them their physical characteristics. "He's immune to it, too."

Hades and Demeter both looked shocked at this development. Gods weren't even immune to charm. Not really. With enough power we could shield ourselves against it, but any one of us could be taken off guard.

"How many of these 'projects' does Zeus have going?" Hades demanded, his tone making it clear he didn't agree with Demeter's word choice.

Demeter shrugged. "Plenty, I'm sure. He wanted to see how long it would take to create new gods through the humans. Looks like he's only a few generations away."

"That's sick!" Melissa exploded. "How can you talk about this like it's some casual thing?"

Demeter drew back in surprise. "I didn't intend—"

"We're *people!*" Melissa snapped, brown eyes blazing. "You don't get to breed us like lab rats, or control us, or make assumptions. What if you're wrong and Zeus wants him dead? That risk is fine with you? I guess he's just human after all. We don't matter much compared to your divine egos."

"Melissa, that's enough!" Demeter snapped.

I raised my eyebrows. I'd never heard Demeter use her mom voice. It was pretty scary.

Melissa knew Demeter better than I did, and she didn't seem nervous, but still, it might be the better call to get her out of here. I looked to Hades for a clue. He seemed distracted. Touching his temples, he looked like his head could be bugging him, but he wasn't quite sure.

Wait. I'd looked away but some detail drew my head back to Hades with a snap. A smear of bright red blood collected under his nose. Hades stared at his bloodied fingers like they belonged to someone else.

"Demeter," I gasped. But her focus was on Melissa.

Melissa narrowed her eyes at Demeter. "I don't answer to you. As far as I'm concerned, the only member of this entire pathetic pantheon who matters is Persephone. The human race is better without the rest of your meddling and manipulations and *disguises!*"

The whole Zeus was Joel revelation hadn't gone over well with her. Adonis touched Melissa's arm and stage whispered, "Not that I don't appreciate it, but don't forget who you're talking to."

Melissa shook him off. "I'm not afraid of them. I'm not the one who needs worship to live."

"Demeter!" Tearing my gaze from Hades wasn't easy. Something was wrong, very, very wrong. Gods didn't bleed. They just didn't. But I'd sworn to protect Melissa, so Hades would just have to wait. If Demeter tried to hurt Melissa there wasn't a whole lot I could do but get in the way. I gulped. I really didn't want to do that.

But Demeter didn't seem bothered by Melissa's outburst at all. She regarded Melissa with a look of exasperated patience. Melissa stared at her for a moment, waiting for some reaction. When none came, she gave a dramatic sigh, flipped her hair, and stormed out of the room. Adonis took a quick look around and followed her.

"Not a word." Demeter held up one finger and regarded me with icy cold eyes. "I'm not interested in your opinion. But you—" she turned to Hades "—I'm surprised you could resist commenting on that little displa—"

She broke off with a surprised gasp. I followed her gaze and felt my stomach twist in fear. This didn't happen. It just didn't happen. Hades lay unconscious in a crumbled heap on the wooden floor in a pool of blood.

Chapter XXIV

Hades

PERSEPHONE'S BREATH was hot in my ear. Her nails dug into my back. My hands ran down her body . . .

"Oh, Hades," she moaned.

"Um . . . Wow." The voice came from across the room.

I pivoted, changing the dreamscape around me. By the time I faced the door, I was standing in my library fully clothed, facing Persephone, the real non-dream version. She stood in the doorway, slack jawed.

"Persephone!" Crossing the room in an instant, I gathered her in my arms, joy and relief rushing through me in equal parts. "Gods!" Her body, whole and solid, fit against mine in a way dreams could never get right. I'd been so worried I'd never hold her again. Never see her again. "Are you okay? Where are you?" When I pulled away, I kept my arms wrapped around her waist because I couldn't bring myself to let go. "Physically, I mean," I added, when she looked confused. Dreamwalking got complex whenever a distinction had to be made between the mind and the body.

She didn't answer. I looked her up and down, gaze snagging on her necklace.

A small green spiky plant hung in a metal basket, the red bud of a flower just beginning to blossom. The glass-blown pomegranate seed that hung from the basket was a token of my realm. It was a perfect conduit, representative of her lineage and marriage with a piece of each realm in one neat package. But that wasn't why she wore it here.

It meant something to her because *I* gave it to her. I meant something to her.

Even after everything that had happened to her because of me, she still went through the trouble of replicating that necklace in her dreams. Clearing my throat, I jerked my gaze away from the necklace. No apparent injuries, but there was no telling if that was reflective of reality or how she saw herself at the moment.

Something was wrong. In my relief I hadn't noticed she failed to return my embrace, but now I saw how rigid she held herself in my arms. There was a look I didn't recognize in her eyes.

Persephone was an open book. I never had to guess how she felt or what she was thinking. It was all right there. But now her expression was guarded. And there was something else in it. Fear.

Of me?

Was I *really* dreaming again? Would she fall to pieces like in that horrible nightmare? No. She was real. She was here. I could feel it. "Persephone?" I reached out to caress her cheek.

She flinched. "Don't." Her green eyes searched my face. "I should be able to tell." Her voice broke. Persephone tried to pull back, but I held her fast.

My arms dropped, and I stepped away for good measure. There was no telling what she had gone through, so if she needed space, I was happy to oblige. "Tell what?" I wanted to reach out to her, to demand to know what Zeus had done and how I could fix it, but I didn't dare. "Persephone." It was a fight to keep my voice calm. "Tell me where to find you."

She looked away and I jerked toward her, almost unable to restrain myself from reaching for her. Persephone flinched.

"Hey, it's okay. Wherever you are, I'm going to find you and bring you home, okay? But I need you to point me in the right direction."

"Stop." She took a deep, shuddering breath, sliding her air plant pendant back and forth on the chain of her necklace. "I should be able to tell him from you. If you're not him, if you've taken that from me, if you've broken us that badly . . ." Iron glinted in her eyes, hard and unfeeling. "Then you won't have to find me. I haven't come into my powers yet, but I will. I'd be afraid of that day if I were you."

Comprehension bubbled up within me like bile. I was going to *make* a way to kill him. Then I'd drag him down to hell and spend the rest of eternity making him suffer.

It wouldn't be enough. It would never be enough. Zeus looked like me. The bastard had looked like me when he'd hurt her. "It's me."

She didn't look convinced, and I didn't blame her. I didn't sound like myself. There was no getting past this. Even if I found a way to get her back, even if everything worked out, she would look at me now and see him.

"Everyone is 'me.'" Persephone put the word in air quotes. "Be more specific."

The hardness in her voice was so foreign to me that I hesitated. Her eyes narrowed, and she shot out her hands, shoving me backward. "Get the fuck out of my head, you sick bastard."

That snapped me out of my reverie. I grabbed her hands. "I'm not in your dream. You're in mine. I promise, I'm Hades. You?" I didn't know. She was acting so different.

"I'm Persephone. Oh gods, Hades!" She half-fell, half-threw herself into my arms. "I'm so sorry, I couldn't tell. I thought it was you, but I couldn't tell."

I shushed her, savoring the feel of her warm body pressed against mine. "It's fine." Gods, it felt good to hold her. "Are you okay?" The force of whatever happened to her had knocked me out. And I was *a lot* stronger than she was.

She shook her head. "I'm not okay, Hades."

My arms tightened around her. "I know. But you will be, when this is all over you're going to be fine. You have to hang on to that, hear me?" I stared into her eyes. "You're not okay, but you will be. We will fix this, I promise. Now, where are you?"

"I escaped Zeus, I think." Her voice was muffled from talking into my shoulder. "I jumped out of his weird cloud castle thing. It's in this hemisphere. It was still daylight when I jumped."

My mouth dropped open. "You jumped?" Zeus' fortress wouldn't be close to the ground. The pain I'd felt had been her shattering upon impact.

She sniffled. "I couldn't . . ." Her breath hitched. "I thought if I jumped I could teleport, but even if I couldn't, anything would be better than what he was doing to me."

Her shoulders shook, and I tightened my embrace. Zeus wasn't dumb enough to leave his offspring with teleportation rights. I had my doubts she'd actually managed to escape him, but we'd cross that bridge when she woke up. "Do you know where you landed?"

The look on her face told me this wasn't going to be good news. "The middle of the ocean."

Poseidon's realm. Shit. I took a deep breath. "Did you swear fealty to Zeus?"

She shook her head. "I tried. Hades, I'm so sorry, I tried, but I made this promise I wouldn't hurt you. So I couldn't do it."

Relief rushed through me, and I immediately felt guilty for it. She couldn't swear fealty. My realm was safe. But what had that cost her?

"I'm sorry," she whispered.

My voice hardened when I asked the next question. "What did he do to you?"

"What did he do to *us*?" she asked, ducking my question. "I can't feel you anymore. I don't know what you're thinking. Did the lightning sever our connection somehow?"

"Impossible." I tilted her head up, lips brushing against hers with tentative patience. I'd let her set the pace. She surged forward, pushing up on her tiptoes and looping an arm around my neck to yank me to her level as her lips crushed against mine with a desperate urgency. Power surged between us, ripping through our connection. It felt like something broken within me had been restored. We were whole again.

Gods! Her whispered thought echoed in my mind. *I was so afraid I'd never feel this again.* Persephone's fingers dug into my back as she clung to me with all her strength and joy, and unbelievably enough, love. She loved *me*. How could she possibly have it in her to feel *happiness* after what she'd been through, much less joy? She was so strong.

No, I'm not, she objected. *I would have sworn to him if I could have, I wanted to give in.*

Anyone would have. There's more to it than that. You *didn't break.*

Persephone didn't get it, but that wasn't surprising. She was young. I'd been around long enough to see the way pain could twist and bend people. How they could buckle under the misery until they had nothing left to them but the horror of what they'd gone through.

I wanted to follow her example. Escape the horror of the situation though a kiss. But I had to know.

May I?

She hesitated, and then I felt her tentative agreement. Her thoughts flooded mine, and I saw all the things Zeus had put her through. The memory of his voice slithered into my thoughts.

"Maybe I should tell you about some of the things he's done. Better yet—" a curved blade appeared in Zeus' hand *"—how about I just show you?"*

The images of what came next, the shallow slashes separating each layer of skin as she cried out for the torment to end, for me to help her, assaulted my mind like blows. My hands tightened around her, and I broke off our kiss. "I'm sorry, I'm so sorry."

"It wasn't you." Her soft lips whispered against mine. Teasing me with their proximity.

I took the bait. I'm only a god after all. Even guilt couldn't stop me from enjoying the way the kiss deepened, or the feel of her body tight against mine. No. I'd sooner slit my throat than hurt her. But I'd given

Zeus ideas, methods to use to torture her. That was almost as bad.

Teeth grazing my bottom lip, Persephone teased images of her mom, Melissa, and the other priestesses from my mind. Her relief coursed through me with the realization that her people were safe.

When Persephone came up for air, she tilted her head. "Where is everything?"

The dreamscape had gone blank. My face heated. I'd been so wrapped up in her, so focused, that for a moment nothing else existed. Drawing on a modicum of power, I formed an image of our library in my mind. Nothing fancy, it was just a general impression of warm colors, rich browns, and earthy reds with bookshelves and big comfortable furniture. I never put much detail into my dreamscapes. Why waste the power? Still, I was careful not to leave out the touches of her influence that were scattered throughout the library. Bright splashes of colors, flowers in vases on the wooden tables.

Persephone smiled. Moving to one of the small wooden tables that lined the walls between shelves, she touched one of the flowers, a bright yellow daffodil. Suddenly, that flower was the brightest, crispest thing in the room. "What's a sympathetic bond?"

I led her to one of the indistinct chairs in the library. "I always thought sympathetic bonds were a myth. Apparently, upon reaching equilibrium, we can feel what the other feels."

Her thoughts flashed to . . . what was that, a pearl? "So if you hurt one of us you hurt both of us?"

"To a diminished degree. I doubt I would have been walking around these last few weeks if I'd felt the full extent of what you experienced."

She considered that. "If I die, what happens to you?"

My heart seized in my chest, not from fear of my own death, but hers. "I'm not going to let that happen."

"But if it did?" she persisted. "If something Zeus does can kill me because I haven't come into my powers, or if my powers burn through me . . . ?"

I shook my head. "It won't kill me." Her mind flashed back to that pearl again. "Persephone, what is this about?"

"Could we maybe talk about that later?" She looked up, green eyes pleading. "I'll explain, I promise, but I just don't want to dwell on any of this right now. I won't ask about your plan or whatever that—" she waved in the direction of the bedroom and I coughed "—was."

"That was you."

She turned pink. "I'm not that flexible. Look, I really don't want to spend this time rehashing everything that's happened to me. I know that's probably not wise, but can we just—"

I kissed her. She was right. We didn't know how much time we had left. She needed time to regroup. To brace herself for whatever was next to come. And me, I just needed to hold her.

A while later I felt her fading beneath my touch.

I'm waking up! Fear saturated her thoughts.

I'll find you.

Chapter XXV

Persephone

I THINK IT WAS my ribs breaking that woke me up. Gasping, my eyes flew open as a sharp pain ripped through my chest. *Hades!*

I'm here. His thoughts felt distracted, and I got the distinct impression he was talking to someone. My vision blurred then focused on a kid's face hovering right above mine. He lifted his head and put his hands to my chest.

Suddenly I had Hades' full attention. His presence flooded my mind so fast I got mental whiplash. I had the strange knowledge he was seeing, hearing, and feeling everything I was.

Weirdness. I pushed Hades' mental presence away so I had room to think and shoved the kid off me. Or tried to. Instead I coughed, water spewed from my lips, and the kid helped me roll to my side.

"Annie, are you okay?" The kid shouted in my ear over and over again.

Gods, he was loud!

I caught my breath and turned to face the mysterious stranger. He looked twelve or thirteen with streaked blond hair hanging haphazardly in his face. A Metallica shirt and jeans with all kinds of holes in them hung off his lanky frame.

I stared at him in complete shock. Where was I? Who was this kid?

"Are you okay, Annie?"

"That's not my name." I took a quick look around the cave we were crouched in.

Despite the darkness, every detail was illuminated, just like in the Underworld where there was no sun but it was somehow always light. Water filled most of the cavern, leaving us in the only dry spot. My dress had turned a dingy gray with black streaks from the slick rocks below me, and I was soaking wet.

He was completely dry.

The kid shrugged and showed me his phone. "It's one of the steps."

I stared at the video through the thick, bulky, waterproof case, now more confused than ever. A woman performed CPR on a child-sized dummy on the screen.

Well, that explains what he was doing.

Had that been my thought or Hades'? The fact I didn't know bothered me, but I pushed my concerns aside. There were more important things to worry about.

"Where am I?" Touching my necklace, I took a mental inventory. I didn't feel *good,* but nothing screamed life-threatening injury.

The boy's eyes flicked back and forth over my face with frank curiosity. "The ocean."

Gee, that narrows it down. That time I knew the thought came from Hades. It seemed our connection was restored even outside of dreamwalking.

Thank the gods, I thought before turning my attention back to the kid. I opened my mouth to demand a more specific answer, then noticed the kid's eyes churning blue and green with streaks of brown and white swirling like tiny waves around his pupils.

"You're Poseidon's son."

He tensed.

"He mentioned you—said he had a son about my age." My age? Apparently the god of the sea couldn't add.

You're closer to his age than Poseidon's, Hades pointed out.

The kid brightened and puffed out his chest. "If he told you that, he must trust you a lot. No one's supposed to know he has a son."

That made sense. The more people who knew he existed, the greater chance of his name getting out there and killing him with worship he wasn't old enough to handle. I grimaced as my ribs knit themselves back together. I was glad to have been unconscious for the bulk of my heal from the fall.

When the pain passed, I returned my attention to the kid. "You saved me."

He didn't save you. It takes more than drowning to kill you, Hades pointed out.

I'm awake, I'm breathing, and I'm not at the bottom of the ocean. Kudos to the kid. Turning my thoughts away from Hades, I focused on the conversation at hand.

"Thank you so much."

He turned bright red. "Aw, it was nothin'. Triton." He stuck out his hand.

"Persephone."

He hadn't taken his eyes off me since I woke up. "You're like me, right?"

"A god, you mean?" I climbed to my feet and glanced around the cave. There wasn't much to see.

He nodded.

"Yes."

"Wow!" The way he stared at me, like I was some sort of new and interesting species, made me uncomfortable.

I pressed my fingers against the wet wall of the cave. It felt odd beneath my hand. Normally when I touched stones or dirt or plants, I felt connected to them, like I'd tapped into some kind of energy. But this . . . felt empty. Foreign. It wasn't my realm. "Surely you've seen a goddess before. What about your mom?"

He looked down, fidgeting with his phone. "You're different." Clearing his throat, he looked up at me through his messy hair. "Why are you here? No offense, but you're not supposed to be here. I can feel it."

I knew exactly what he meant. Since I wasn't invited to this realm, it felt like it was trying to push me out. The menacing water lapped on the rocks and the walls of the cave felt like they were bearing down on me. "I escaped from another god. If you could just point me toward land . . . "

"You're a long way off."

I clutched at my necklace. I'd been afraid of that.

"But don't worry. I can call my father—"

"No!"

Triton looked up at me in alarm, and I forced myself to smile.

"I mean, I'd rather not involve anyone if I don't have to. The other god . . ." *is maybe only a little worse than your dad.*

I couldn't say that. Poseidon was an ass and a pervert. He'd harassed and raped my mom centuries back when she'd spurned his advances. Supposedly he felt bad about it now, and he'd told me he wanted to help me when I was dying on his beach, but I'd rather die than put my mom in the position of having to be grateful to that jerk.

Still, however screwed up Poseidon was, his kid was sweet. "It's kind of complicated."

Triton wrinkled his nose. "It's political stuff, huh?"

I considered. That could work. Zeus, Poseidon, my mom, and Hades were all realm rulers. Anything involving them had ramifications. "Isn't everything?"

"I can take you to land. And"—he reached up and put a hand on my shoulder, a faint blush covering his face—"I can protect you from that other god. I'm stronger than I look."

Having a guide would be helpful.

But what if Zeus found me? Could I really justify putting this kid in danger?

It's worse than that, I realized, horrified. This wasn't just some kid. He was Poseidon's son. Zeus would want him for the same reason he wanted me. We both had a natural right to realms he didn't control.

Zeus would torture him like he'd tortured me, and when, not if, Triton broke, Zeus would have access to this realm and be that much harder to defeat.

That would suck, but it was the thought of Zeus torturing this happy, smiling, adorable kid that filled my gut with dread.

"I'll find my own way, thanks."

Triton gave me a skeptical look, eyes sparkling in challenge. He lifted his chin and with a confident grin demanded, "What are you gonna do? Swim?"

I opened my mouth to reply and realized I didn't have the slightest clue how to get home.

"Yeah, I thought so." Triton's voice was thick with satisfaction. "You're stuck with me, like it or not."

Chapter XXVI

Aphrodite

HADES WOULD LIVE.

Between the two of us, Demeter and I propped him up on the couch and cleaned most of the blood off his face—ugh, nose blood. Gross. He was still out cold, and Demeter was on edge. No doubt wondering what had happened to Persephone to reverberate to Hades like that.

I shuddered to think of it. Gods shouldn't bleed. Stopping outside of Persephone's room, I raised my hand to knock on the door.

" . . . just saying that was thoughtless," Orpheus said from within the room.

I froze.

"I refuse to be afraid of them," Melissa snapped.

I looked up and down the hall. No one was there. Shrugging, I pressed my ear against the door.

"That's your first mistake," Orpheus retorted. "But fine, don't be afraid. Would it kill you to show a little humanity? Her daughter is missing—"

"Gosh, I missed that memo."

I smirked. It was nice not being on the receiving end of Melissa's snark.

"Look, I get it. She's your best friend, and you're scared and worried. But multiply that times infinity for Demeter. We're lucky she hasn't scorched the earth looking for Persephone. We're *extremely* lucky she's not pointing fingers. In case you haven't noticed, deities aren't the most mentally stable people, so the least you could do is not *bait* one who's barely holding it together."

I frowned. Yes, he had a point, but I didn't like my mental stability being impugned upon by some half-breed. These crazy people kept acting like humanity was something to aspire to. Did they read newspapers? Humans were crazier than the gods had ever been.

I heard a thud, like something banged hard against the nightstand. "I hate her." Melissa's voice was so soft I could barely hear her.

"I don't think you do."

"Having fun?" A voice whispered in my ear.

I jumped a foot off the ground with an embarrassing, pathetic-sounding squeak.

"Easy now." Ares laughed and put his arm around my shoulder to steady me. I jolted at the sensation of cold leather brushing against my bare arms.

Speaking of arms—wow, his were firm! I gave him a subtle once-over and tried to recover what dignity I could. Melissa was busy, and I was bored.

He caught my look and grinned. "Need a distraction?"

I leaned forward, pressing my body against his, balancing on my tip-toes, and whispered, lips brushing against his ear, "I could use a change of scenery."

His arms dropped to my waist. "I'll take you wherever you want."

I slipped out of his embrace and flashed him a smile. "Great, I'll get the keys." I giggled at his confused look. "You did say anywhere. Let's go recruit Hephaestus."

He gave me a withering look. "Not what I had in mind."

I tossed my hair over my shoulder. "*You* should have been more specific."

Chapter XXVII

Hades

I WOKE TO A COLD appraisal from Athena's gray eyes. Disoriented, I sat up and realized I was in Demeter's living room.

Hades! Persephone's fear sliced through me.

I'm here, I assured her before turning my attention back to Athena. "Can I help you?" I laced the sentence with as much sarcasm as I could muster.

It wasn't much. Whatever just happened to Persephone had left me shaken. Pain was not an experience I relished, especially hers. I pushed my hair out of my face and narrowed my eyes at Athena.

"You need a haircut," she observed.

My attention snapped back to Persephone as she struggled to get out from under . . . who was that kid and what the hell did he think he was doing?

CPR. An ally then.

"You're up." Demeter walked into the room. Her face was pale and drawn with worry.

I swung my feet over the couch and sat up. "We don't have a lot of time."

"Is she okay?" Demeter demanded.

The ocean, the kid chirped.

Gee, that narrows it down. I stood, taking a deep breath to steady myself as the room shifted around me. "She seems to have escaped Zeus."

Athena's expression became guarded, and I exchanged glances with Demeter. We all knew it wasn't likely she'd escaped. Zeus was up to something.

You're Poseidon's son, Persephone exclaimed.

I swore. But how! How could he have known she'd find some random, unknown child of Poseidon?

Unless . . .

"Could Zeus have access to a prophet?" I asked while Persephone got worked up about Poseidon saying Triton was her age. *You're closer to his age than Poseidon's.* I didn't add how relieved I was that Poseidon saw Persephone as a child. Or that I wondered what it said about me that I didn't.

You saved me, she said to the child-god.

No, he didn't, I objected. It was irrational to feel defensive, but that didn't seem to matter. Twice now someone from Poseidon's world had saved her when I couldn't. *It takes more than drowning to kill you.*

" . . . not aware of any living prophets, divine or otherwise." Athena leaned back in her chair.

I jerked my head up. "What?"

She frowned at me. "Are you all right?"

With effort, I turned my attention away from Persephone. She was safe. I was no good to her if I couldn't focus. But when I opened my mouth, I realized I couldn't answer Athena's question because I wasn't "all right." I'd seen what Zeus had put her through, and it wasn't over yet. "Can you repeat whatever you just said?"

She let out a long breath, as though repeating herself was beneath her. "I am not aware of any living prophets."

Prophet gods were rare, even before Olympus fell. Knowing the future impacted the outcome, and gods, even minor ones, tended to be involved in events in a big way. Most gods born with the gift of prophecy passed it along to demigods eons ago. Humans rarely lived long enough to master it. It had taken Cassandra centuries to get to the point where she could understand her visions, much less communicate them to me in any meaningful way. It was unlikely Zeus had access to a prophet.

But it made so much sense. Over the last year we'd been moved around like pawns until we were exactly where Zeus wanted us. I thought back to the day I'd rescued Persephone and brought her down to the Underworld. Could that have all been engineered by Zeus?

He couldn't have known how everything would end up, could he?

"Demeter . . ." I paused, uncertain how to proceed. "Persephone is in Poseidon's realm."

Demeter's face went white.

"He hasn't found her yet, but—"

Demeter grabbed my hand, and before I could blink, we were standing on a beach. She walked to the edge of the shoreline, picked up a shell, and tossed it into the ocean.

"I can handle this." I kept my eyes on the ocean and off her face, sensing that she needed a moment to compose herself. "You didn't have to come."

"Yes, I did." Demeter's skirt and hair whipped around her in the wind. She looked so much like Persephone, but I never saw Persephone in her. I'd known Demeter too long, I supposed.

"You ever think we were better off before we rebelled?" Demeter asked.

"What do you mean?"

She shrugged, eyes searching the waves. "Look at what's become of us. All of us, estranged and half dead for want of worship. At least in the before, in the void, we had one another. We were happy sometimes, weren't we?"

Before Zeus. "Only because of you." I sat down on the sand and draped my arm over my knee. "You held us together, kept us sane."

The sound of the surf crashing against the sand all but drowned out her next question. "You blame me, don't you?"

Demeter had all but disappeared into her realm after Zeus declared himself the god king. We'd been so happy to be free of the Titans. Then we'd discovered a tyrant far worse.

"I blame him." I scowled out at the water, remembering Zeus' first offense on what would become a very long list.

She shook her head. "I was the oldest, I should have seen what Zeus—"

"We all should have known better. He fooled us all, Demeter."

"Did he? Or did he change after he killed Cronus? He never seemed unstable before their death, but afterward . . . he was manic at times."

The sun disappeared behind a cloud, casting us in shadow, and my thoughts went to Aphrodite's plan. "We're not going to let that happen to her. Demeter, I have an idea."

"I've heard, and I support it. But I have my own plan, and if things progress far enough that my plan becomes necessary, it won't be me you need help from to implement yours."

Understanding dawned on me, and I slammed my mind closed around the realization before Persephone could follow my train of thought. "Demeter, no!"

"She would never forgive us if we risked our realms to save her. This way she has a chance."

More than a chance. "But Demeter—"

Her green eyes turned on me, boring through to my very soul. "You won't tell her."

I didn't keep things from Persephone. I was the only person in her life she could say that about, and I wasn't going to change that now.

Demeter seemed to see that and sighed. "It's a last resort."

"Let's not let things get that far."

The water rippled, then Poseidon, the shirtless wonder, appeared before us.

"Demeter," he breathed. He didn't seem to notice me. I suppressed the urge to roll my eyes. Was the man ever fully clothed?

"Where is she?" Demeter's voice was low and dangerous.

Poseidon looked at me, confused. "Demeter, I—"

"Don't!" Demeter charged forward, feet splashing in the surf as she lunged at Poseidon. "No equivocation, no double meanings. You know *everything* that goes on in your realm. I remember. Where is my *daughter?*"

Poseidon looked stricken. "I'm so sorry. I thought she reached Hades in time. I tried to help, but she knew about . . . about us, and she wouldn't trust me."

"You think she should *trust* you?" Demeter demanded, eyes blazing. The wind whipped her blond hair across her face, and she pushed it out of the way with an impatient flick of her wrist. "What do you mean you think she reached Hades in time? We know she's in your realm. Take me to her immediately!"

"She made an entrance to the Underworld—"

"Demeter, he doesn't know where she is." I edged toward the shore. I wasn't willing to set foot in Poseidon's realm but was ready to grab Demeter if I had to.

"He just said he saw her!"

"He's talking about something else." I'd forgotten Poseidon had tried to help Persephone when Thanatos attacked her. She'd made an entrance to the Underworld and crashed in the library, battered and broken. The thought of her half dead in my arms . . .

I shoved my hair out of my face and filled Poseidon in on everything that had happened since Persephone left his sight.

"I'm not getting involved," he declared.

Demeter pursed her lips into a thin line. "If he takes over, it will affect your realm just as much as ours."

"Maybe for the better. He's not going to be satisfied with the worship of dead souls. He'll do something to make humans worship the gods again."

"Probably," I agreed. "A cataclysm, a flood, or some other massive destructive force. People will die—"

"What use are people to me unless they believe in us? I won't hurt your wife, Hades, but I won't help her either." He looked at Demeter. "I'm sorry."

She glared at him. "I've thought you many things Poseidon but never a coward."

"Call me whatever you like, Demeter. I'm not dragging my realm into this."

"Then give us permission to enter your realm so we can find her," I demanded. "You can still be neutral, though it won't save you from Zeus."

"*She's* always welcome in my realm." Poseidon inclined his head toward Demeter. "Always has been, always will be. You? Not so much. Good luck. I hope you find her." The water rippled around Poseidon as he vanished.

Demeter stared at the spot where Poseidon had been standing. Then she got a look on her face I recognized. It was the same look Persephone had when she was about to do something stupid.

"Don't." I stepped forward and grabbed her arm. The waves crept closer to us, so I pulled her farther up the shore. "You're not going into his realm."

Demeter's face hardened, and she looked up at me, squinting in the bright sunlight. "She needs me."

"No, she doesn't."

Demeter narrowed her eyes.

I continued, speaking fast. "He's promised not to interfere. He won't hurt her, he won't turn her over to Zeus—"

"There are other dangers!" Demeter strained toward the ocean, and I knew she'd be off in a second if I let her go.

"Damn it!" I tightened my grip, and pulled her closer to me. "Think about it for a minute! Zeus can't get to her in Poseidon's realm. Can you say the same for yours?"

Demeter shook her head, still pulling away from me. But I knew she was listening, otherwise I'd have a tree growing through me right now. Unless she was conserving all her power to help her daughter and didn't consider me a threat yet. I kept an eye on the ground, scanning for any random plant growth.

Demeter's lips pressed together in a frown. "She'll be safer in your realm."

That's why she hadn't lashed out. She needed me to keep Persephone safe. "If she's lost, they can't ask her to fight Zeus."

Comprehension dawned on her face. A small army of gods waited in Demeter's living room for one purpose. To kill Zeus. It had to happen. Otherwise Persephone, and pretty much the rest of the world, would never be safe. But it wouldn't be an easy fight.

Persephone didn't have to get caught up in all that.

"There are other dangers," Demeter repeated.

"She can handle them." That wasn't easy to say. My impulse was to protect Persephone from everything, but every time I'd tried to shield her in the past, I'd ended up shoving her into more danger than before. When she faced Boreas alone she'd returned unscathed. She'd gone up against Thanatos and turned every one of his Reapers against him. And she'd survived Zeus. Persephone wasn't helpless. I had to trust she'd find her way back to me.

Was I making the wrong choice? What if this was what Cassandra hadn't been able to tell me about? If she'd seen something bad, then I shouldn't go with my first impulse because that would be the outcome she'd see. Or would it? No. I couldn't think about prophecy too much or it might self-fulfill.

I'll be fine. Just take care of my mom.

Persephone's voice snapped me out of my thoughts. I'd forgotten she could hear me.

She could take care of herself. I had to trust that or I'd drive myself crazy.

Chapter XXVIII

Persephone

I COULDN'T DO IT anymore. I'd put up with a lot in the last year. The gods were real. Sure, I could accept that. The fact that I was one of them was a bit tougher to swallow, but why not? I'd been stalked by a season. Weird, but hey, these things happen. I became Queen of the Underworld. Whatever, the closet alone was worth it. But I'd finally hit my absolute limit. The thing I couldn't believe no matter what else I knew was possible. This was too much to swallow.

I remembered my first thought when I'd met Hades in the Underworld, and I thought I was in a coma or something. That Melissa and I were in a car crash on our way to the Orpheus concert. Everything made sense before that trip. Reality hadn't yet broken down.

That was it. It had to be it. If I could just make myself wake up, life would go back to normal.

I hoped my car was okay.

"You've been awfully quiet." The water stirred where Triton swam alongside the carriage, pushing against the bubble that kept me breathing.

I didn't look at him. I didn't look at anything other than my own hands folded in my lap. He wasn't real. Mermaids were *not* real. Neither was the dolphin pulling me along under the water in a fricken carriage. Or the bubble that protected me from the pressure of the ocean and provided air so I could breathe.

Nope. I didn't believe it. Not for a second. I was in the hospital or a mental ward. Either one. I just needed to snap out of it and go back to reality.

Was a reality without Hades worth going back to?

"I can go back to human legs if you want," Triton offered. "It's just easier to swim this way."

"Of course it is." I forced myself to smile, but I still couldn't turn to look at him. "'Cause you're a mermaid."

"Merman," he corrected for the hundredth time. If he heard the hysterical edge to my voice, he didn't seem to notice. "I'm no maid. Look, see. No sea shells." There was laughter in his voice. "I promise not to let any of the fish sing around you if that helps."

I kept my eyes on my hands, refusing to take in my surroundings. I was done. Finished. I'd played the goddess game long enough. It'd been a nice dream . . . sort of, but I was ready to wake up now.

Wake up, I commanded myself. *Now.*

You're not dreaming. Hades sounded tired of this train of thought.

Says the voice in my head. How reassuring.

Hades sighed and fell silent, leaving me alone with my muddled thoughts.

"You think I'm a freak, don't you?" Triton slipped into my bubble, dropping into the seat beside me with a thud. He'd shifted back to regular legs. Thank the gods.

"What?" I turned to look at him, forcing myself to tune into my surroundings. Coma or not, there was no reason to hurt anyone's feelings. "Sorry, it's not you." And it wasn't. Technically if he was a manifestation of my inner psychosis, then it was completely me. "I'm just feeling a bit . . . overwhelmed. It's been a long day." I'd jumped out of a castle in the sky and landed smack dab in the middle of a Disney cartoon. Long day didn't even begin to cover it.

Triton studied me for a minute, and I marveled at how much he looked like his father. Was this how people who knew my mom felt when they looked at me? "So . . ." I ventured, setting aside my convictions that I was in a coma for a minute. The knowledge wasn't helping me. I wasn't waking up. Since I was stuck, I had to play this out. "What's it like living down here? It must be pretty lonely."

"Nah, there's tons of us." Triton brightened at the chance to talk. "Mostly old men, but there are nymphs too."

"You still have nymphs down here?" I slid my necklace back and forth on the chain. "They mostly died out on the surface."

"The fall of Olympus didn't hurt us as much as it did you. The residents of my dad's realm still believe in everyone, you know?"

I nodded. It had worked out the same way in the Underworld. Hades lost a chunk of power with the fall of the gods, and some of the lesser known deities of the Underworld had died, but the souls living in the Underworld who walked and talked with the gods every day believed enough to keep it running pretty much the same.

Worship from the dead wasn't as strong as worship from the living, but it didn't have an expiration date. That was why Zeus wanted to take over the Underworld so badly. It was a land that wouldn't die.

I braved a look out of the carriage. The ocean passed by in a whir of motion. It was dim, but not as dark as I thought it would be. The sunlight filtered down and reflected off the white sand. Coral forests lined both sides of the road we were traveling, but here and there I could peek through the reef and see what looked like small domes with various kinds of creatures swimming to and fro.

If this were set up like the Underworld, I'd say we were in the suburbs. I hadn't seen anyone else on this road other than us, but the path seemed well traveled.

It was kind of pretty down here. As long as the bubble around me stayed right where it was. I shuddered at the thought of drowning. I'd never liked swimming, much less the ocean. The fear was instinctual. This wasn't my realm. The entire atmosphere made it known I wasn't welcome. My stomach had been twisted in knots ever since I'd woken up down here, and I suspected it was going to remain that way until I left.

"It's boring though." Triton fidgeted in his seat. "My dad's so strict. He won't even let me leave the circle—"

"Circle?"

Triton chattered away, not seeming to notice my question. "And not even just me. He's super bossy to everyone. It's like we're in North Korea or something and you have to hang up a picture of your leader. I mean what is—oh, yeah, the circle? You'll see when we surface. It's like a safe zone for sentient residents. Anyway, so my dad . . . "

I blinked, trying to keep up with the rapid pace of conversation, but he'd lost me at North Korea.

"I mean, it's like throwing an egg at a house and expecting the house to crack. Who does that? And he expects me to be all, 'Yes sir, and no sir,' but I'm a god too, so shouldn't *he* be treating me with some respect?"

Hades tuned in for a minute. *He's still talking?* He groaned and tuned right back out.

"It's weird, right?" Triton asked.

I blinked and nodded. "So weird."

"Totally! Like, unicorn in space weird. He's got to have one of those tumors in his head from screaming so much."

"Wait!" I put up a hand as if that would stop the endless flow of prattle. "There are unicorns?"

Triton gave me a look generally reserved for small children and lunatics. "Um, no. It's just a saying."

My shoulders sagged in disappointment. "Oh."

"So, what's your realm like?"

I opened my mouth, but before I could answer, he bombarded me with questions about my realm, the people in it, celebrity gossip, and video games. The inquisition lasted for what felt like hours before the carriage came to an abrupt halt.

"Oh, we're here!" Triton stepped out of the carriage and motioned for some green seaweedish looking people, very obviously female, but beyond that indistinguishable, to take the reins. I stepped out of the carriage, making sure my bubble stayed around me.

"Where's here?"

"The sand bar. There's an island above us, we just have to swim a little tiny bit. I'll be right here with you."

"We're surfacing?" My thoughts shifted to Zeus. "I can't be seen until I touch land." If I were in my mom's realm, I could teleport before Zeus could grab me. But if he saw me first . . .

"No one can find you here." Triton touched my shoulder. "Don't worry. I'll protect you. Now take a breath."

I drew in a deep breath just before the bubble popped. Triton grabbed my arm, and kicking off the sandy bottom, we swam up to the surface. It wasn't far. Once we surfaced, he led me toward a shoreline, and within seconds we could stand and walk.

When I looked up, I realized why Triton wasn't worried about Zeus seeing me. There was no sky. Just more ocean. I could see dark forms swimming through the waves above us and took a shaking breath.

"This is the circle," Triton announced. He took my hand and helped me to shore while I looked around in shock. I could swear I felt sun. It was blindingly bright outside, but it couldn't be.

Just like the Underworld, Hades reminded me.

Right. Not real sun. And this . . . area . . . must be shielded. That explained the air, and the random land and trees, and . . . was that a bird I heard? The sand beneath my feet didn't feel familiar at all. There was no resonance, no life in it that spoke to me. This was land, but it wasn't my realm.

Don't over think it, Hades warned. *I don't want to go down the coma road again. Look, we created your realm and the Underworld. Why not an entire realm beneath the ocean where your human scientists can never find it?*

"What's that?" I asked, pointing to the horizon. A thin strip of land was just barely visible, almost too far away to see.

"An edge of the circle." Triton steered my eyes to the end of each line of sight.

"Land surrounds all this water on every side." He motioned to the ocean we'd just emerged from. "Any water inside this circle of land is safe. And the land is . . . mostly safe. But everything on the *other* side of the circle is visible to your people. Anything semi-sentient lives here, either on the land or in the water, or both. Everything else . . . "

A thick line of rainforest-like trees lined the entire shore. I heard jungle noises and squinted to get a better look, but the tree line was too thick to see through. "How far from regular water are we?"

Triton bit his lip. "Pretty far. It'll take a week or two to hike from this end to the other."

A week. I fiddled with my necklace. That wasn't so bad. "And then? How far from land that's not part of your realm?"

Triton shrugged. "I've never been. But we can travel faster once we hit water."

"And there are . . . things . . . in the other water." Images of sharks and giant octopi filled my mind. I was terrified of the ocean.

"They won't mess with you while I'm here." Triton beamed. "I told you, I'll protect you."

"Okay." I took a deep breath and tried to push aside my unease. "Let's go."

I started toward the tree line, and Triton grabbed my hand. "Not that way." A flicker of fear flashed in his eyes.

"Why not?"

"That's where the giants live."

Chapter XXIX

Aphrodite

"I STILL CAN'T believe you tricked me." Ares' hands were clenched tight to the black leather steering wheel.

I looked at him over my sunglasses. "I can't believe you were that easy to trick. Hey, can I ask you something?"

"Might as well," he grumbled.

"Why does everyone think I'm easy?"

Ares considered for a moment, and my opinion of him rose. He wasn't stammering excuses or flushing in shame or acting indignant. Gods, I decided, were much better at handling this question than humans.

At least the humans I'd asked.

"Wishful thinking?" He suggested with a shrug. "With the exception of that stunt in the hallway, I haven't gotten any mixed signals. Probably has something to do with your charm."

"I can control my charm."

"I can too, but *most* people still find me irresistible. Just because you have it under control doesn't mean people can't sense you're awesome." He gave me a sideways grin. "Are you?"

"Awesome?"

"Easy. 'Cause when we get back from this . . ." He trailed off with a suggestive look.

I grinned and pushed my sunglasses over my eyes. "Guess you'll just have to stick around and find out."

Ares studied me before turning his attention to the road. "Why doesn't anyone trust you?"

I gave a bitter laugh. "Because I'm working with Zeus."

Ares turned his head so fast he nearly lost control of the car.

"Oh please, not willingly." I examined my nails so I wouldn't have to see his face when he put that little puzzle together.

It felt like an eternity passed before he spoke again. "Well, that sucks."

I laughed. "You're telling me."

He pulled the car to a stop. I glanced around. We were parked outside of a square brick building with faded posters of old video games hanging from the windows. "Here?" I waved my hand at the abandoned arcade. "Seriously?"

Ares shrugged. "You can still turn back."

I got out of the car and walked up to the dingy windows. They were yellow with pollen, making it impossible to see inside.

Ares pounded on the door, frowning when the pollen rained down on his hand. "What season is it here?"

His question gave me pause as I wondered where he came from. That, and I found myself stumped, realizing how *much* time had passed. "Uh . . ." I did some quick mental math. "Winter? Yeah, it's what? Mid-December?"

"So . . ." Ares shook the pollen off his hand. "Is it safe to assume this is old, or has Demeter just completely lost track of the seasons?"

I shrugged. "This is Georgia. It's never safe to assume anything about the weather here." I didn't know if it was the concentration of nature deities in the area or just an unfortunate location, but just because it was nearly eighty degrees outside now didn't mean it wouldn't be snowing tomorrow.

Ares knocked again, lacing it with enough power to shake the building. "I know you're in there!"

"Go away!" A gruff voice shouted back.

"Aw, hell." Ares clenched his fist and flames sprang up from his flesh. He touched his hand to the glass, and it shattered.

"That's—" I started.

"Awesome?" Ares interrupted, flashing me a grin.

"Not how glass reacts to fire." I finished, staring at the pellets of glass covering the sidewalk.

Ares frowned at me and started to say something, but was cut off when a huge hulking shape burst from the arcade screaming obscenities and tackled him.

Ares lit up like a match, flames encasing his body like the top of a baked Alaska. The man punching the daylights out of Ares was undaunted by the fire.

"Knock it off!" I pulled at the big guy's shoulder. Fire licked my arm and I yelped, surprised by the unexpected pain. The man, Hephaestus, I realized, spun around at my touch and raised his hand as if he were going to hit me, then froze.

I shifted uncomfortably under his intense stare.

"Yeah, she's pretty. Now get *off* me." Ares pushed at the bigger man until he relented. "You okay?"

He grabbed my hand, which was taking its sweet time healing. A pulse of power passed through me, speeding up the process, but I hardly noticed.

Hephaestus stood, towering above me, but that wasn't what made me step back in fear.

Half of his face was an unrecognizable web of scar tissue. It looked melted. Skin hung in odd places. His empty eye socket drooped toward his nose. Like one of those Photoshop tricks where you click the mouse, and an image swirls into a grotesque parody of its former self.

"What happened to you?" I gasped. Gods could heal from anything, so what could possibly disfigure a deity? I couldn't tear my eyes away from his face. It rippled, like a current of electricity was passing under his skin.

"I took my weapons back."

I shuddered as images of the long metal stakes bombarded my mind. Once upon a time, he'd created a weapon that could kill gods with a scratch, but they'd all been melted down centuries ago.

"I've told you a hundred thousand times," he continued, glowering at Ares, "I don't make them anymore. Bringing her along to charm me into it is just low."

"I didn't—" Ares started.

"Hey!" Hephaestus called, but it was too late. I'd slipped into the arcade and was looking around wide-eyed.

The arcade was *really* nice inside. Sure there were posters of video games plastered all over the walls, but the place had a sleek, modern look that appealed to me. The furniture was beautiful. Everything was made of hand-worked metal. I paused at a large table. Metal, of course, but it was like nothing I'd ever seen before. A myriad of colors—bronze, gold, silver, and every metallic shade in between—wove together to create a spectacular pattern of leaves. I felt like I was touching fall. I'd half expected bunk beds and empty pizza boxes, but this . . .

Of course the furniture was nothing compared to the tech. One wall showed a picture of heavily-armored, computer-generated people fighting some big red fiery . . . something. But the picture was moving. I tilted my head, searching the seamless wall for a screen. Glancing up, I followed a pattern of lights to a projector attached to the ceiling. The espresso-colored sofa on a wrought-iron frame was littered with keyboards, mice, and random game controllers.

"Dude! Heals? Where are you?" A nasally voice demanding answers drifted from the wireless headset perched on the ottoman.

"Get out!" Hephaestus growled, grabbing me by the shoulder and turning me around. "I didn't say you could come in here."

"Your teammates are dying." I pointed to the wall.

He cursed and snatched his keyboard off the couch, typing at a rapid pace. I watched him play for a minute.

"Course that's nothing compared to the death and destruction we're going to see if Zeus gets his way." I crossed my arms and moved in front of the wall.

Hephaestus paused, a scowl further twisting his mutilated face

I dropped my hands to my sides. "We were hoping you could help us."

Fire sparked in Hephaestus' eye. "I don't make weapons anymore!"

"We have weapons," Ares interjected from the door.

I looked at him. "We do?"

Ares grinned. "You've got me, don't you? Plus that chick everyone keeps jabbering on about. Demeter's daughter, what's-her-face."

I rolled my eyes and turned my attention back to Hephaestus. "We don't need your weapons. We need you and every god left. Zeus is powerful, and if we're going to have any hope of winning . . ." I grabbed his hand, giving him a desperate look. If we didn't defeat Zeus, I was done for. "Please. Help us."

He started to object, but I squeezed his hand and looked him straight in the eyes . . . erm, eye, making sure not to flinch.

"Please." I didn't dare use charm. I didn't want him to come looking for me later thinking he'd been coerced into helping.

Hephaestus looked at my hand for a moment, and his gaze softened. Then he looked into my eyes, really looked into them, with an expression I'd only ever seen on Hades' face. Like he could see through me. But unlike Hades, he seemed to like what he saw. After considering for a long moment, he nodded, putting his other hand on top of mine. "Okay."

He didn't let go of my hand until Ares cleared his throat. "Right," Hephaestus muttered, shoving past Ares and walking to the car. "I'm driving."

What was it with gods and their inability to let anyone else drive?

Ares shot me a questioning look. "Did you charm him?"

I tossed my hair back. "Not in the way you're thinking." I didn't have to use charm to wrap a man, god or no, around my finger. He was mine, hook, line, and sinker.

Chapter XXX

Persephone

I CRASHED THROUGH the trees, Triton right on my heels.

"Run! Run! Run!" Triton urged.

I was a good runner. I'd spent most of the last year running, so I'd had plenty of practice. But no matter how fast I was, I couldn't outrun giants. "You said the giants were the other way!" I gasped.

"I got mixed up, okay? Sorry!"

So much for having a useful tour guide. A tree splintered behind me. I ducked as the bark flew at me like shrapnel. Triton cried out and I spun. My eyes widened when I saw a piece of bark as thick as my wrist protruding from his side.

I stared at Triton for a moment, shocked into stillness. Running was out.

Triton looked from the wood, to me, and back again, eyes wide. I didn't know what to do. His knees gave out beneath him, and he sank to the ground, looking more surprised than hurt, but I knew firsthand the benefits of adrenaline. He'd feel it soon enough. The giant thundered closer, the ground shaking beneath me, and I did what I'd always done in a crisis. Shoved aside the terror and acted on instinct.

Throwing up a shield, I channeled more and more power into it until I thought I would burst from the effort. When the mud-streaked giant hit the wall of energy, I twisted it, pulling the shield around him like a net. I'd seen Hades do this to pin down a Reaper who dared attack me.

It was harder than it looked.

The giant howled with rage. Seconds ticked by where I could do nothing but stare at the grotesque beast. His skin stretched over his colossal frame, pulled so tight it looked as thin and see-through as tissue paper. With every breath the giant took, I worried his skin would split open. I felt sick looking at him.

"What did you just do?" Triton stared at the frozen giant in wonder.

Sweat poured down my face as the giant struggled against the shield. Surely there was an easier way to do this, but my knowledge was limited. Wrenching the shield in half, I brought the giant down to his knees. He still towered above me like a tree, but I could look up and meet his eyes.

"Stop struggling." I poured every bit of my charm into that order. Fury and terror added weight to my voice, forging it into a force so strong the giant might have listened without the charm.

But I wasn't going to take that chance.

The giant stopped.

"Persephone," Triton whimpered.

Right. I shook myself free of the horror and disgust and addressed the giant with a firm voice. "I'm going to release the shield. Do not move."

With baited breath, I dropped the shield. The thunder of splitting trees and stomping feet vibrated through the forest as the rest of the giants approached. "Tell them you don't know where we are. Protect us."

The giant nodded. I pulled Triton behind the giant's right foot and cast another shield, blocking us from sight and sound.

"Okay." I knelt beside Triton and touched the tree branch. A sheen of sweat covered his forehead.

"It hurts," he whimpered.

The giants gathered around us, eclipsing the sun. They spoke in a guttural language, shaking the earth with their gesturing. *Please let me be able to fix this.* I took a deep breath and yanked the bark free from Triton's flesh, flinching when he yelled and writhed, his fingers digging violent gouges into the ground. He hit the edge of the shield with a thud. I gritted my teeth against the strain of keeping the giant charmed and the shield in place.

My hands were slick with blood, sweat, and desperation. Triton stopped struggling, eyes going glassy.

"No, you don't." I pulled more power through me, and Triton's flesh knit together beneath my hand. My vision blurred.

When the giants thundered out of the clearing, the charmed one stayed behind. Dropping the shield, I told him, "Go, and forget your part in this." The ground shook as he walked away. I counted to a hundred before dropping the charm.

"Thanks!" Triton stared at me wide-eyed. "You're . . . How did you do all that at once?"

I shook my head, too relieved to care how I'd pulled that off, and struggled to my feet, clutching my necklace like a lifeline. "Let's find somewhere safe for the night, 'kay?"

"Safe, huh?" Triton offered me his hand. "How do you feel about safe-ish?"

Chapter XXXI

Aphrodite

"YOU WENT WITHOUT me?" Melissa exclaimed. She'd pulled me into Persephone's room the minute I'd finished showing Hephaestus around and making introductions. "I thought we had an understanding."

"You were busy with Orpheus." I yawned, flopping down on Persephone's papasan chair decorated with yet another flower pattern.

Melissa muttered something under her breath and snatched a fresh shirt from her bag. She changed clothes like five times a day now that we were sharing a roof with so many hot guys. They were fun to look at. I couldn't tell if Melissa was trying to impress them with her vast wardrobe, or if she was just frustrated that they seemed unimpressed and was not going to give up until she found an outfit that demanded their notice. Either way, I don't know why she bothered. She could run around naked and they probably wouldn't react. That was no reflection on her. Gods and nymphs go way back, but she was under Demeter's protection, and no one would risk losing rights to live in this realm for a mere nymph.

"You should have waited." She shimmied into a new skirt.

A deep, dark bruise just below her collarbone caught my eye, and I bolted upright. "Is that what I think it is?"

Melissa flushed, covering the hickey with her hand. "It's not your business."

I pretended to be scandalized. "He's married!"

"Oh, don't be stupid!" Melissa snapped, shoving a silky shirt over her head. "I wouldn't make out with Orpheus."

"Aw, come on. I'm not going to judge you for getting some action while your best friend is missing." *Might put you in a better mood,* I thought, though the idea of Melissa being happy and *not* whining all the time was unimaginable. What would she talk about?

Melissa ignored my teasing, but I wasn't letting her off the hook that easy. Not after the hard time she'd given me. Plus, I was really curious

111

who would want to make out with Melissa. Who would risk pissing off Demeter? Adonis, maybe?

A flash of envy passed through me, but I suppressed it. I wasn't interested in Adonis.

"Aw, come on, who's the lucky guy?"

"Joel," she snapped.

My smile froze. "Sorry, what?"

"This isn't new. I had it when I died, and now it's never, *ever* going away. Happy?"

My mouth hung open like I was some kind of slack-jawed idiot. Melissa looked close to tears. I scrambled for something to say to make her feel better. "He always had a thing for nymphs."

Melissa laughed, but it sounded more like a sob. She swiped at her eyes angrily and turned her back to me, taking deep breaths.

"Why didn't you say anything when she got back? I don't think she would have spent so much time with him had she known—"

"Gee, that makes me feel *much* better. What was I supposed to tell her?" Melissa's voice was thick. "Hey, Persephone, thanks for bringing me back from the dead and all, but while you were stuck in the Underworld, fearing for your life, I was having a blast here on the surface with the guy you've been crushing on all year."

"She had Hades," I pointed out. "It wasn't like she was thinking about Joel while she was down there."

"He didn't talk to me after . . ." She trailed off, gathering her hair into a ponytail at the base of her neck. "I thought it was me. Boreas had me for a while, and then I was dealing with the whole coming back to life thing. It wasn't until school started that I even tried to track him down, and by then he'd moved on. Gods, I was so stupid. I *was* worried about Persephone when she was down in the Underworld. But . . . I was also relieved. Everything in my life revolved around her, and for the first time, I was free of it."

Melissa shook her head. "You don't know what it's like to have your whole life spelled out for you, and I couldn't even be mad at her because she didn't know. She's my best friend. I love her like a sister, but she's my obligation. And I thought he—"

Her eyes closed. "Whatever, I was wrong. He was just keeping tabs on me to use against her. I make a good hostage."

I nodded. "You really do."

Melissa rolled her eyes. "Yeah, thanks."

"Did he charm you?"

She grabbed a white wooden brush—with yellow daisies carved and painted in an intricate pattern running up the handle—from Persephone's dresser. "No. I think I'm immune. Persephone's never charmed me, and as much as I'd like to think it's because I'm her best friend, I watched her come into her charm. She had *no* control over it."

Immunity could be handy. "Don't tell anyone else." Melissa would make an ideal spy in a room full of Zeus' offspring who were used to charming mortals into forgetting what they'd just heard. "When Persephone gets back, she can try to charm you to confirm, but you're probably right. Nymphs had a higher tolerance to that kind of thing."

"Mmm," she agreed, pulling her hair up into a ponytail and twisting a purple scrunchie into place. "I think that makes it worse though. That I wasn't charmed. I don't have that excuse, you know, for not being able to see through him. For being tricked, or whatever. It was all me."

"Worse." Any sympathy I felt for her vanished. Something in my voice must have sounded off, because Melissa stopped fiddling with her hair and studied my reflection in the mirror.

I let out a disgusted sigh. "You know, every time I think I'm starting to like you, that you're not just beneath me, you open your mouth and something stupid falls out."

Indignation flashed in Melissa's eyes but I continued, heedless of her rage. "You have no idea, none, what it's like not to have a choice. To *have* to listen and obey. To feel your body controlled by someone else, moved around like a puppet, and to be absolutely *powerless* to stop it—"

"Aphrodite." Her voice was low and sympathetic.

I rolled my eyes and turned away from her, grabbing the brush and yanking it through my own hair. "I mean—" I sighed, exasperated. "Just think of how poor Persephone felt."

"Persephone?" She said it slowly, like she wasn't following.

"Yeah. He was totally charming her, like the whole time he was Joel."

She was silent for what felt like an eternity. Then just when I was sure the silence was about to become something real, something that could break and shatter, she cleared her throat. "You're right. That must have been terrible. I wasn't thinking." Her hand touched my shoulder, a quick, quiet gesture of comfort, and I sucked in my breath.

I could count on one hand the number of times someone had touched me with any measure of kindness in my entire life.

"Not surprising for a nymph," I muttered, putting the brush down on the dresser. "Anyway"—I kept my voice bright—"don't ruin it. You had a nice time with a boy you liked. It was exciting and special, and *you* chose it. Don't let all the crap that came later ruin that for you."

She nodded.

"Hey, want to do something useful?" I asked.

"Like what?"

"We could recruit Poseidon."

Melissa considered for a minute then shrugged. "Yeah, sure, why not."

Chapter XXXII

Hades

IT TOOK ME A while to calm down enough to sleep, but it didn't take long to find her once I'd drifted off.

"You're wanted at a meeting," I told Persephone, after giving her a long kiss.

She gave me an odd look and fiddled with her necklace, a nervous gesture. "Am I in trouble?"

The vision of a principal's office flashing through her mind made me laugh. "No."

"You sounded pretty serious."

"Yeah well, we've got everyone together, so it's time to move on with our plan. Only there's some disagreement as to what we do next."

She weaved her fingers through mine. "Let's go then."

I closed my eyes and the dream shifted. When I opened them we stood in the middle of nothing. Featureless walls closed us in, blending in with the natural oblivion of an unfocused dreamscape. It's hard to agree on a neutral dreamspace for this many gods.

When Persephone saw the sheer number of gods that had gathered, she let out a soft exclamation of surprise. Every living deity left in creation except Zeus and Aphrodite crowded together in the dreamscape. There were just some things we couldn't risk Aphrodite knowing.

"Took you long enough." Apollo leaned against the wall, arms crossed.

Demeter ran forward and threw her arms around Persephone. "Gods!" Her voice was choked with emotion. "How I've missed you."

Persephone clung to her mother with equal fervor, tears shimmering in her eyes. "Mom!"

The other gods looked down or away, giving them time before we got down to business.

"So, how do we kill Zeus?" Apollo asked, breaking the moment. "And by we, I mean all of *us.*" His gesture took in all of Zeus' children.

"Because really, we're the only ones who can."

"And if she's escaped, how do we find him?" Athena's cold gray eyes studied Persephone with an intensity that made me nervous.

"If?" Persephone interrupted.

"That shouldn't be a problem." Artemis tightened her sleek black ponytail before cracking her knuckles. "Zeus is hunting all of us down. We just need bait."

"He's too smart to take any of us as bait," Ares interjected. "We have to assume he knows we've already grouped up."

"He does," Persephone confirmed, her hand returning to her necklace, sliding it back and forth along the chain.

I offered her my hand before anyone else could notice the nervous gesture. I didn't want this group knowing all my wife's tells.

"Not her." Hephaestus pointed to Persephone. "He's looking for her anyway. If he were to find her—"

"Not an option," I growled, stepping in front of Persephone.

Arguments erupted from the other gods.

"It's a sound plan!" Athena argued.

"Her! You're not serious!" Apollo stepped away from the wall, giving Athena an incredulous look. "She's just a kid."

"She's Zeus' blood as much as any of us are," Thalia pointed out.

"I *said* it's not an option!" I looked to Demeter for support, but she was strangely silent.

"I'm *not* swearing my power over to a teenager," Artemis interjected. "No offense." She tilted her head toward Persephone. "But we all have much more experience fighting than you do."

"Which is why Zeus will see any one of us coming." Hephaestus' mouth twitched on one side, wrinkling his mutated flesh. "But he needs her for his plan to work, so we don't have to find him if we use her. He'll do all the work for us."

"Hey!" Persephone yelled over everyone else. "Don't I get any say in this?"

"No." I turned to her. "You don't understand what they're asking."

"Then someone better start explaining," she snapped. Everyone was still yelling back and forth to each other, so she pitched her voice louder. "If I don't know what's going on, I can't help. If I can't help, I'm not wasting my time listening to this. *I* still need sleep, you know."

"They want you to kill Zeus." Athena's voice was patient.

Persephone's eyes widened. "Kill him?" She laughed. "Me? How?"

"We'd all swear fealty to you. You'll have enough power if we all pitch in." Ares looked Persephone up and down and shoved his hands into the pockets of his leather jacket. He at least had the grace to look uncomfortable with what he was suggesting.

"I haven't even come into *my* powers yet!" she objected.

"How are you not dead?" Artemis asked. "You've been away from Hades for weeks now, and you're . . . *really* powerful. I can feel it. If you haven't come into your powers, then how?"

I'd been wondering the same thing.

"I've been using them up." Persephone shrugged, tucking her blond hair behind her ears. "Easy enough when you're at death's door every five minutes. That doesn't mean I can channel all of yours."

"Not for long," Hephaestus pointed out. "But maybe long enough to defeat Zeus."

"I'd die."

Hephaestus shrugged. "If that's what it takes to eliminate Zeus, it's worth it."

I crossed the room in a flash and slammed Hephaestus into a wall. Black veins crisscrossed over his face, expanding into a spider web as they burst. He gasped, pulling at my arm.

"Hades!" Ares tried to pull me back.

I dropped Hephaestus with a thud. "Anyone else want to suggest my wife commit suicide?"

No one spoke.

"I'll kill Zeus," Ares volunteered.

"He'll be expecting *you*," Athena pointed out.

"If we find Persephone first—" Demeter clasped her hands in front of her and waited until she had everyone's attention "—then we could ambush him. This doesn't have to be a solo mission. We may not be able to kill Zeus, but we're more than capable of holding him down while one of you does the job."

"Where's Poseidon?" Persephone looked around like she just noticed he wasn't there.

"He won't help," Demeter said.

"We'll see about that," Persephone muttered.

I felt her willing Poseidon to come here. She put a ton of power behind it. The hair raised on the back of my neck. The other gods exchanged alarmed glances. Persephone really was too strong. Between the power she was born to, half of both Thanatos' powers, and mine and all the worship she'd garnered thanks to Orpheus and his wife Eurydice, she was a force to be reckoned with. If she could actually control it all without endangering herself, she'd have a shot against Zeus.

Not happening.

"Gods! Can't you people take a hint? I'm staying out of this!" Poseidon appeared next to Persephone, for once, wearing a shirt.

"Nice pajamas." I smirked at his teal silk get-up, half surprised he wasn't wearing a nightcap.

"Don't you have some cradles to rob?" Poseidon snapped.

"Enough. We *have* to defeat Zeus," Persephone said, cutting to the chase as usual. "Your generation let him get this far out of control. You owe it to us to help."

That raised more than a few eyebrows. I just grinned. Persephone was a political nightmare, but she had a way of getting things done.

I loved my wife.

"No," Poseidon growled. "I'm not bringing my realm into this."

"You owe me." Persephone's green eyes flashed.

"I owe *her*." Poseidon pointed to Demeter. "Last I heard, you'd rather die than accept my help."

Persephone shrugged. "This is bigger than I am."

"Tough. I'm still not dragging my realm into this."

Too late I saw her thoughts.

"I have your son."

Poseidon's face went dark with rage. "Excuse me?"

Stepping between them, I kept my eyes level with his. I had to hand it to her, I was impressed. But this didn't sound like the Persephone I knew.

"I'm not threatening him!" Persephone sounded offended. "But he's with me. Zeus is looking for me. What do you think is going to happen if Zeus finds me?"

"You tell him to come home *now!*" Poseidon was shaking with rage.

"I've told him to. A couple of times. He won't leave." Persephone's face colored, making it obvious to everyone in the room *why* the prepubescent brat wouldn't leave the gorgeous goddess.

Poseidon swore. He seemed to age before my eyes. "If he is harmed in *any* way—"

"I will do *everything* in my power to protect him."

I winced. Poseidon studied her for a moment, neck craned to see her around me.

"I'll find you and deliver you safely to shore—"

"To me." I clarified. "Don't you dare just abandon her on the shore."

"Fine," Poseidon growled. "I'll deliver you to Hades—"

"The god, not the place," I added.

He rolled his eyes. "The god, not the place, unharmed by my hand."

"*Hands*, feet, weapon, or any other extension of self, including divine powers."

"Oh for Chaos' sake, Hades, I'm not going to hurt her!"

"Nor will any of your agents." I kept my eyes locked with his. There was no way in hell I was leaving a loophole.

Poseidon rolled his eyes, but repeated addenda after addenda for the next several minutes. "Satisfied?"

"Not yet," Persephone said.

"What?" Poseidon narrowed his eyes at her.

"I don't have to be easy to find," Persephone pointed out. "The longer it takes to find me, the longer it takes to find him."

Poseidon glared at her with such intensity that I reached behind me to push her backward. She refused to move.

"Fine," he spat. "I'll throw in my support against Zeus. I suppose you want fealty?"

"At some point," she replied.

I turned to look at her, impressed and incredulous. *You're you?* I asked, just to clarify.

I'm Persephone, no tricks. For better or worse. Her heart pounded, and her stomach churned.

You're not evil. I assured her, knowing where her thoughts lay. *We need as much power behind us as possible. What you're doing is—*

I know. That doesn't make it right.

"Fine." Poseidon raked his hands through his spiky blond hair. "I'll swear to you *if* you promise to break the bond as soon as Zeus is dead and return all my power to me."

"I promise."

Poseidon looked between the two of us. "There's a rumor you two have hit equilibrium."

"That's not your business," I said.

Poseidon grinned. "That sympathetic bond's a bitch, huh?" Before I could blink, a trident appeared in his hand, and he shoved it through my gut in a swift motion.

Persephone cried out behind me. I grunted and grabbed his hand, forcing his flesh and bone to wither at my touch. Grimacing, Poseidon pulled the trident free. Persephone gasped, crumbling to the ground, clutching at her stomach.

"Threaten my son again," he said, "and I'll *find* a way to put you down for good."

He vanished.

Chapter XXXIII

Persephone

A HAND CLAPPED over my mouth, and my eyes flew open. My throat felt raw from screaming, and my stomach blazed with pain.

Triton's worried face hovered above mine. He searched my eyes for a minute then removed his hand from my mouth. "What happened?"

I opened my mouth to tell him *exactly* what happened but stopped. What would I accomplish by telling Triton his dad was a jerk who went around stabbing people with tridents? Plus, he was under the impression Poseidon trusted me. What if he left me in the circle? There was no way I could navigate this place on my own.

My stomach twisted with guilt. I was using him. He was just a cute, friendly kid, and I was using him to get through the circle and to get Poseidon's help. Triton seemed to relish the adventure, but putting him in danger made me sick. We'd only been in the circle for a few days, and I'd already met more frightening creatures than I ever cared to encounter again.

Guess I really am a goddess now, I thought. *Manipulating people like pawns. And what other choice did you have?* Hades asked.

Shaking my head, I refused to even consider that line of logic. I couldn't think like that. If I put enough thought into it, I could justify *anything*, but that wouldn't make it right. Triton didn't deserve this.

A woman's scream echoed in the distance, and Triton winced. "Get ready to move."

I got up, dusting the dirt off my dingy gray skirt. The skirt was in tatters, not exactly ideal for running through the forest.

Another scream. This one closer.

"Who is that? Is someone in trouble?"

Triton shushed me and stared up at the sky, finger to his lips. A black shadow burst through the canopy of leaves above us with a shriek. I caught a glimpse of wings, claws, and a flash of red hair before Triton grabbed my hand. We ran, tripping over branches.

"Harpies!" Triton yelled. "They eat—"

"People?" I guessed. Most things in the circle seemed to. "Your realm sucks!"

"My realm?" He grinned at me. "You have bears, lions, and dinosaurs, and *my* realm sucks?"

I started to explain that dinosaurs weren't really a thing anymore, but the harpy dove again. Oh gods, instead of the claws of a bird it had hands with razor sharp nails. Catching hold of my hair, it yanked me toward the tree line. Quick as a thought, Triton grabbed a branch and swung it at the harpy. It shrieked and flew backward, and I was running again.

"This wa—WHOA!" Triton yelped, dropping out of sight.

Suddenly the ground dropped from below my feet. The harpy shrieked. I slid over Triton, and together we tumbled to a stop at the bottom of the hill.

For a second neither one of us moved, just lay there catching our breath, then Triton lifted his head, looking down at me with an impish grin on his face.

"That's one way to lose a harpy."

I laughed despite myself and swatted at him. "Get off!"

Triton looked down, realized he was sprawled out on top of me, and turned bright red. "Sorry!"

He looked at me for a moment, gaze dropping to my mouth.

"Triton—" I shifted underneath him and tried to wriggle free. "Move."

"Right, right, sorry!" He got up and looked up the hill. "Looks like we lost her."

Nodding, I climbed to my feet with a mental groan. I'd seen that look before.

He liked me. That made this whole thing even more complicated. Not only was I using him, but in his mind I was probably stringing him along. I needed a nice way to say, "not happening, kid." Even without Hades in the picture, Triton was *way* too young.

Oh, I don't know, Hades teased. *I keep hearing age isn't that important.*

Shut up. I glanced at Triton, and he looked away. The tips of his ears turned red.

Feels awkward, huh?

This isn't funny, Hades.

Not to you, he agreed.

I ignored him. "You okay?" I asked Triton.

He nodded. "Just trying to get my bearings. I think if we walk west we should hit the end of the circle soon."

"Let's find a place to sleep and get back to walking tomorrow," I suggested. Poseidon would find us soon, and then this whole ordeal would be over, but Triton didn't have to know his dad was looking for us yet. Backup, just in case Poseidon found a way to weasel out of the deal.

I closed my eyes against the wave of guilt that washed over me. I was just as bad as the rest of the gods.

Chapter XXXIV

Aphrodite

"THAT COULD HAVE gone better." I squeezed the ocean water, slimy with seaweed, out of my hair, letting it puddle onto the wooden floor in Persephone's room.

"How were we supposed to know Persephone already got him on board," Melissa grumbled. She kicked off her shoes and poured water out of them. "I need a shower."

"We're lucky he didn't do worse than drench us. I heard she really pissed him off." I stepped in front of the mirror, closed my eyes, and concentrated. When I opened them, I was in a new outfit with perfect hair. "Much better."

"That's so unfair."

I tapped her shoulder. When she turned around she wore a designer outfit and makeup. "Better," I decided. "But not your color." I tapped her again, changing her shirt to a deep purple.

"Thanks," she said grudgingly.

"Knock, knock," Adonis called, rapping on the door as it opened.

"What is wrong with you? We could have been changing!" Melissa snapped. Her cheeks pinked when she saw Adonis though, and she didn't sound all that angry.

"Sorry." He started to close the door, but Ares caught it.

"Hey ladies."

Hephaestus and Apollo came in on Ares' heels.

"What is this? Central station?" Melissa grumbled.

Hephaestus shrugged. "I need to avoid Hades for a while."

"Why?" I asked.

"We can't get into that here." Ares gave me an apologetic look. "But for the record, I agree with you, man." He glanced over his shoulder to Hephaestus and flashed him a grin. "It would make sure there wasn't another Zeus anyway, and would get everyone's powers back."

"No one should hold that many realms," Apollo agreed.

Melissa started to say something, so I elbowed her. She whirled on me, brown eyes flashing. I gave her a look that said, *"Shut up and let them tell us everything."*

At least that's what I hoped it said. Whatever message she got from it, she kept her mouth shut.

"I just needed to get away from Demeter." Adonis glanced between Melissa and me. "She keeps watching me like I'm a science experiment that needs to be dissected."

"I'm bored," Ares said. "You two seem to be having all the adventures."

"Yeah." Apollo grinned at me and gave me a slow once-over. "I'd rather be where the action is."

I tossed my hair behind my shoulder. "Oh, as if." I pursed my lips and looked around the room. So many hot guys, so little time.

My gaze snagged on Hephaestus, and my throat went dry. I think it was the side of his face that wasn't scarred that threw me for a loop. What he should have looked like.

Could Zeus do that to me? Would he? Or would he just make me swear over all my powers until I died? What if we did win, but Persephone died? Demeter *hated* me, Hades would go nuts with grief, and neither one of them would forget my part in Persephone's capture.

I cleared my throat. "But you're right. The less time we spend around all of them—" I motioned toward the door "—the better."

Chapter XXXV

Hades

DEATH WOULD BE too good for Poseidon. It had been almost twenty-four hours since he stabbed me with that asinine trident, and I was still seeing red. The wound healed immediately, but the message had been sent. Nearly every god who was left knew how to hurt me now.

They could use her.

I rounded the corner of the staircase and ran straight into Demeter. She held a finger to her lips and pointed to the kitchen.

" . . . expecting her to be that powerful," Athena murmured.

"She's stronger than *I am*," Apollo said.

"She's stronger than all of us combined, except for maybe Aphrodite," Ares interjected.

"Leave me out of this. All I can do is charm, remember?"

Ares laughed. "Baby, with the level of charm you've got, that's enough."

"How much power did Demeter give her?" Artemis wondered.

Hephaestus snorted. "Forget Demeter. Hades . . . "

" . . . heard she killed Boreas and Thanatos." That was from a voice too soft for me to recognize.

" . . . fealty first."

" . . . two realms . . ." Artemis' voice floated down the hall.

"Three if she could get Zeus to swear," Athena added.

Aphrodite's voice rang out, pitched higher than the rest like she wanted me to hear. "She couldn't survive any of our fealty. She hasn't come into her powers yet. That's why we're using someone else. Right?"

In the silence that followed, I heard the refrigerator door open and close. A glass clinked against the countertop.

"We can't really go into that with you." Ares sounded apologetic.

"We should use her." Athena again. A chair squeaked as it slid across the wooden floor.

"Don't let Hades hear you say that," Hephaestus warned.

"She'd die," Ares said at the same time.

"Good," Athena said. "Don't look at me like that. You were all thinking it. When Zeus took down Cronus, he became almost as bad as they were. When Cronus killed Uranus, it was the same thing. Ditto for Uranus killing Chaos. We're stuck in this cycle of sending our youngest most promising fighter after a brutal tyrant and we keep being surprised when he wins and takes over. She's strong enough to become the next Zeus if we let her, and I for one don't want that to happen. If she dies killing Zeus, it breaks the cycle."

I clenched my jaw and stepped toward the kitchen, but Demeter shook her head, stopping me.

"If we want to break the cycle, shouldn't we *not* send our youngest most promising fighter this round? Why don't we do something different? Athena, you're the oldest. Why don't you give it a whirl?" Laughter was evident in Ares' voice.

"Sending Persephone only solves our problem because she can't possibly survive the fight."

"I shouldn't be hearing this," Aphrodite said. "Besides, I'm bored. Surely there are more demigods to rescue or something."

"I need to check on my people," Apollo said.

"Hey Demeter! Hades!" Aphrodite raised her voice. "Has anyone seen them?"

"Not since the trident incident." That soft voice again, so low I had trouble hearing it. Who *was* that?

I waited a beat before calling "Yeah?" and walking into the kitchen. There was nothing in their faces to suggest they'd just been talking about sacrificing a seventeen-year-old girl so they could all continue to live freely. It was an effort to keep my voice even, but I managed. Aphrodite met my gaze with a knowing glance, and I suspected I had her to thank for the conversation happening unshielded in the kitchen. Charm could be subtle.

"I'm so bored." She gave me a flirtatious smile. "Are there any other gods or demigods or *anything* for me to track down?"

"Want to track a prophet?" Zeus kept manipulating us like chess pieces on a board, but his moves were too good. No mortal prophet would have enough experience to predict anything useful, but an immortal prophet would do the trick. I knew of one, but couldn't for the life of me remember his name.

Demeter walked into the kitchen and grabbed a pitcher of water from the refrigerator. "Did someone call for me?"

"Can you teleport me home?" Apollo asked. "I keep getting calls from my people—" He broke off at Demeter's withering stare, then seemed to find the courage to continue. "I just need to explain that I'll be gone for a bit. They get antsy when they don't know where I am."

"Tiresias." I remembered. "Zeus gave him immortality, right?"

"That old pervert?" Athena demanded. "He's immortal?"

"Wait, the cross dresser?" Ares asked at the same time.

"He's completely insane. There's no way Zeus would be able to get anything useful out of him," Apollo said.

"Beats sitting around here doing nothing." Aphrodite tossed her red hair over her shoulder with a grin. "I'll find him."

"I'm going," Melissa announced.

I turned, surprised. I hadn't noticed her sitting at the table.

"Me too," Ares, Adonis, and Hephaestus said at the same time.

"He's not far from my church," Apollo added.

I'd forgotten Apollo was Tiresias' patron. Demeter and I exchanged glances. He hadn't always treated his prophets well. It would be easier to talk to Tiresias without him, and if Apollo planned to return to his church with any kind of fanfare, maybe Tiresias wouldn't see Aphrodite coming for him. Because the gift of prophecy came from Apollo, the visions were biased. Cassandra told me once she hadn't even seen the Trojan War coming because she kept having visions of Apollo crashing his new chariot.

"You should have a service," Demeter suggested.

"Really?" Apollo sounded surprised.

"Oh yeah, that's a great idea," I agreed. "Tell them what's going on. We need worship now more than ever if we're going to overpower Zeus." I spoke without a trace of sarcasm. We *did* need the worship. Orpheus had been writing blogs and doing interviews and concerts all over the place to try to bring our levels up. Apollo's followers would only help.

"Then shouldn't they be praying to me?" Ares asked. "Since, you know, I'll be the one fighting him."

"If they pray to Apollo, and he swears his powers over to you, it shouldn't make a difference." Artemis' voice was low, and she looked at me with laughter sparkling in her eyes. I knew how she felt. Apollo having his own cult of drugged-out hippies was never going to stop being funny.

"Hey, yeah!" Apollo enthused. "We'll have, like, a really *big* service. Let me go get it all set up."

Demeter smiled. "There's safety in numbers. I'll come with you. Hades?"

"We can come," Artemis volunteered, grabbing Ryan's hand. "I'd love to see your—" she snickered "—church."

Ryan shrugged. "Um, sure."

I studied him for a minute. He'd taken the news of Artemis' divinity pretty well. Most humans needed more time to process our existence than he did. I shoved my hair out of my face. "I need to swing by the Underworld and check in. But I'll catch up with you guys then."

Demeter nodded, then turned her attention to Melissa. "I'm granting you travel rights for one trip. Take Ares, Hephaestus, Adonis, and Aphrodite. Find him, and come straight back, no detours. Don't let anyone wander off. Anything happens, contact me."

"Okay," Melissa agreed.

Demeter motioned for them to hold hands, tapped Melissa's shoulder, and they vanished. Then she took hold of Artemis, Ryan, and Apollo, and they teleported to the church.

Once everyone else was gone, I studied Athena for a long minute, letting all the anger I'd felt during the overheard conversation heat my gaze.

Athena shifted under my gaze and cleared her throat. "She's brave, your wife."

I didn't so much as blink. "She's stronger than she looks."

Athena nodded. "With Poseidon on our side, we have a shot. Zeus may actually die by the end of this."

"*Everyone* dies eventually." I inclined my head toward her. "And if they're really, really lucky, they haven't done anything to piss me off."

Chapter XXXVI

Aphrodite

"HE'S NOT HERE." I ran down the stairs to the lobby of the massive house the prophet resided in with a pair of his red heels in my hand. What? It wasn't like he was coming back, and they were just my size.

"Gee, you think maybe the prophet saw us coming?" Melissa said dryly.

Ares barked a surprised sounding laugh. "You're kind of funny for a human."

I had a bad feeling. We didn't mean the prophet any harm, so why flee? Glancing around, I took in the signs of the prophet's hurry—a half-eaten lunch still warm on the kitchen table, a smattering of hangers covering the floor of the closet like he'd snatched clothes at random, and the unlocked door when we entered. What had he seen?

And why had he run?

"And you're way too easily impressed," Hephaestus muttered. Adonis nodded in agreement.

"Aw, come on!" Ares said, still laughing. "Saw us coming, because he's a prophet, it's—"

"As good a guess as any," said a voice as smooth as silk from the doorway.

I blanched. Zeus.

At the sound of Zeus' voice, Ares swore and turned, pushing Melissa and Adonis behind him.

"Charm them and tell them to hold still," Zeus told me with a grin.

My body moved of its own accord, turning and meeting each of their eyes. They all froze, even Adonis and Melissa. I did a double take. Adonis' eyes locked to mine, pupils still normal sized, unlike everyone else. *Just go with it,* his look seemed to say.

I swallowed hard and tore my gaze from him to Melissa. She stared back at me, eyes wide with fear. *Please don't move.* Zeus didn't know I'd sworn not to charm Melissa. Maybe she could teleport and get away.

"Now ask them to swear fealty to me," Zeus instructed.

No. I wouldn't do that. He couldn't make me. I clamped my mouth shut.

Gods. Words rose in me, filled my mouth, and pushed against my lips. Swallowing, I forced them down, but they tore at my throat. A strangled, keening wail filled the room, sounding so alien, so desperate and helpless, that at first I didn't place it as mine. I wouldn't do this to them. Zeus would kill them in an instant. I wouldn't—couldn't—*Stop!*

My lips parted of their own volition, and I clapped my hand over my mouth. Zeus crossed his arms, looking bored. I couldn't resist forever, and he knew it. Every fiber in my being pulled at me to obey his command.

I looked away from Zeus, but found I couldn't face the blind devotion in Ares' and Hephaestus' eyes. They had nothing left of themselves in their expressions. All they wanted to do was please me. This was wrong. My vision blurred, and I blinked away the tears, looking to Adonis instead. His bravery and strength was telegraphed in his stiff posture and the trust in the eyes he kept glued to my face.

He trusted me! No one trusted me. A small smile formed on his face, cool and confident. *Just wait,* it seemed to say. *We'll get out of this.*

No, I wouldn't do this. Not to him. Not to Melissa or any of the others. They trusted me, maybe even thought of me as a friend, and friendships were precious because they hadn't come easily. I would die before I let Zeus take them from me. Despite my conviction, my jaw stretched, struggling to free itself from behind my tightly clamped hand. But my teeth came together with a click, filling my mouth with the copper taste of blood.

I wouldn't do it. I'd die first. In fact . . .

Hades, I thought desperately. Something moved, but I couldn't make it out from behind the sheen of tears filling my eyes. *I swear—*

In a whoosh I was on the ground, and Adonis was on top of me. "Melissa, now!" Adonis gave me an apologetic look and slammed my head into the floor. My vision flickered. A bright light flashed. Then the acrid scent of burnt flesh filled my nostrils.

I tried to sit up, tried to scream, but instead I fell, slipped, slid into a tunnel of empty darkness.

Chapter XXXVII

Persephone

"I NEED A BREAK," Triton gasped, leaning against the bubble, legs twitching with fatigue. "There's a cave over there." He motioned vaguely, and our weird air bubble floated toward it.

Again? Keeping the frustration off my face was as useless as trying to keep Glinda the Good Fairy out of my head as we traveled along the ocean floor by bubble. I wasn't frustrated with Triton. I was frustrated for him. He couldn't take much more of this. We needed to find land from my realm, real land, soon.

Triton didn't seem to notice. We surfaced in a cave, and he managed a few steps before curling up on the ground and falling asleep. Chewing on my lower lip, I took in Triton's ashen pallor in concern. This wasn't good. Triton hadn't come into his powers yet, and unlike me, he didn't have an excess to burn off. We were making *very* slow time in our quest for land, but more important than that, Triton looked positively sick. I didn't think he could handle this much longer.

If only there were some way to channel power to him safely.

I waited, hoping for a suggestion from Hades, but he seemed *really* distracted. More than that, he'd thrown a wall up between our minds. *Why would he do that?* It wasn't like Hades to keep things from me.

Triton shifted, returning my attention to the problem at hand. Could I do the bubble thing? I threw up a shield and took a few tentative steps toward the water before hitting the edge of it. No good. Shields were stationary, so it didn't move when I did.

Fiddling with my necklace, I tried to recast the shield as I walked. Still no good. The shield enclosed everything within it, including the water. There had to be a way to replicate Triton's bubble. When I'd asked him before, he hadn't been able to explain what he was doing. His bubble seemed as innate as my charm.

Which means I probably can't make one anymore than he could charm someone, I realized.

Okay, so plan "B." How could I safely give him some of my power? Hades could filter mine, but that was because we were married. And marrying Triton was out. Even if marrying Triton wasn't out, it was out.

I could ask him to swear fealty to me. The thought turned my stomach. If Poseidon discovered I allowed his kid to swear fealty to me, he'd make good on his threat to find a way to kill me. Even if I did plan on breaking the bond as soon as we hit land.

Where was Poseidon anyway? I left a chunk of my air plant necklace behind every time we stopped like a trail of glowing breadcrumbs. My plant didn't exactly glow, but the necklace was kind of a conduit to my realm. It would attract Poseidon's attention just by the wrongness of it being here. I'd feel sorry for the poor plant if I couldn't replenish its missing leaves. But if there was one thing I could do, it was grow flowers.

I sat down and leaned against the cold, wet wall of the cave. Would it work the other way around? Could I swear fealty to Triton without my power killing him? I didn't like the idea, if only because I already felt like I was leading the poor kid on. No telling what sort of mixed signals swearing fealty would send. But if we kept moving at this pace, I wouldn't get home this century.

I considered for a moment, then shook my head. I'd have to ask Hades. I didn't know enough about it. In the meantime, I'd wait on Poseidon.

Surely it wouldn't take him too much more time to find us.

Chapter XXXVIII

Hades

FIRE. IT WAS ALL around me. Smoke filled my lungs and the horrible scent of burnt hair assaulted my nose. The sounds of people screaming and crying surrounded me between blasts of piercing sirens. I whirled around, squinting my eyes to see through the burning smoke. Had I teleported to the wrong place? No. There was no mistaking that trashy church sign.

"Sir!" A firefighter grabbed me and steered me toward the large red truck. "You must move behind the line. Were you in the church, sir?"

He sounded doubtful. I didn't look much like Apollo's followers. When I shook my head, he directed me out of his way. Powerful blasts of water spewed from large yellow hoses, and the flames gradually died down to smoldering embers. Working my way through the crowd, I searched for Demeter, Apollo, and Artemis. What had happened here?

Apollo's followers wandered around the smoldering remains of the church, seemingly oblivious to the sirens wailing and the EMTs rushing about, trying to herd them to safety. The rest of the cult lay scattered through the remains of the church, burnt to a crisp.

"What happened here?" I grabbed a bikini-clad girl by the shoulders. "Where's Ap—Mr. Sunshine?"

Her eyes were red rimmed from crying. Or maybe it was something else. "The bad man made him say the magic words that turned him to dust." She took a deep shuddering breath and then burst into tears.

Shock. Wonderful. I led her to one of the EMTs and continued my search. Behind me the girl who had been screaming nonstop changed gears and started singing an altered version of "You Are My Sunshine."

I swore. If, and it was a very big if, what this girl had described was even half accurate, Zeus had forced Apollo to swear fealty. But how had he known where to find him?

I glanced at the church sign. Well, it wasn't like Apollo had been subtle. We shouldn't have let him come back here. But where were

Demeter and Athena?

I grabbed the next teenager I passed. "There were two women who came back with Mr. Sunshine. One of them was blond, nearly my height—"

The boy nodded, looking shaken. "And the hot Indian chick, right?"

I'd never heard Artemis described that way, but sure. "Where are they?"

"They vanished, man."

My blood froze. "What do you mean vanished?" The boy didn't answer and my voice rose. "Vanished like Apollo—er, Mr. Sunshine? Or just disappeared?" Why was I wasting my time with this kid? There were only two options.

I teleported back to Demeter's and was nearly run over by Adonis carrying Aphrodite. Her hair draped over Adonis' arm, almost touching the floor. The red was shocking against her sheet-white skin.

"What happened?" I demanded. "What the hell is going on?"

"You have to go back!" Melissa shouted from somewhere behind Adonis.

Adonis moved past me toward the living room, and I saw Melissa in tears. She launched herself at a bewildered looking Demeter.

Demeter, thank the gods. The tension in my chest eased, and I scanned the room for Artemis. She was curled up on the love seat with Ryan, face streaked with tears.

Demeter shushed Melissa and wrapped her arms around her. "What happened?"

Adonis and Melissa started talking at the same time. "Zeus was waiting for us—"

"He made Aphrodite charm everyone—"

"Didn't work on Adonis—"

"I had to knock her out. She was going to make them swear fealty."

"They told us to go—"

"I didn't have a choice." Adonis looked pale and shaken.

Melissa was sobbing so much it was getting hard to understand her. "I grabbed the two of them and teleported, but Ares and Hephaestus are still there! You have to go back! Please, Demeter!"

Aphrodite stirred, and Adonis sprang into action, grabbing a lamp off the end table. He raised it above Aphrodite, and I darted between the two of them.

"What the hell are you doing?"

"I'll get them," Demeter said. She vanished before I could object.

"If she wakes up, she'll try to charm them into swearing fealty again," Adonis explained. "He never told her to stop. She has to listen to him, doesn't she?"

"Yeah, but gods! Don't hit her!" I didn't like Aphrodite much, but I wasn't about to watch her get beaten to a bloody pulp every time she moved. She stirred again, and I turned, hand brushing back the hair on her forehead. A surge of power flowed from me to her, and she stopped moving.

I made a mental note to thank Hypnos for teaching me that trick. With any luck, she'd be out for a while.

Demeter popped back into the room along with Ares and Hephaestus. They seemed remarkably unscathed. As if reading my thoughts, Ares shrugged and pulled on the sleeves of his jacket.

"Zeus ported out as soon as Hephaestus and I charged him. I think he'd prefer to pick us off one by one."

"I think it may have had something to do with Ares lighting him on fire," Hephaestus added dryly. "Shame it didn't last." His lips twisted in what might have been a smile. It was hard to tell on his face.

Ares shrugged again. "Is Aphrodite okay?"

"What. Happened?" I demanded, catching Demeter's eyes.

"Zeus was at the church, waiting for us. We got out. Apollo didn't."

I opened my mouth to demand to know why Demeter, one of the strongest deities left, had run when she had Zeus outnumbered three to one, but she shook her head, then inclined it toward the couch where Artemis was sobbing into Ryan's shoulder.

I let out my breath. Ryan could be charmed and used against Artemis. There had been an entire congregation of hostages who could be used against Apollo. All it took were two words and one second of weakness to swear fealty to Zeus. It was lucky Demeter got Artemis out of there before Zeus became even more powerful than he already was.

He must have gone straight from the church to the prophet's, which at least answered *that* question. There was no way he could have known our group would be in both places without prophecy.

Unless we had a mole.

The door opened, slamming into the wall so hard the doorknob punctured the sheetrock, leaving a gaping, dusty hole. I blinked, my mind not accepting the image of Poseidon, the shirtless surfer in bright blue board shorts, existing in Demeter's living room.

He closed the door with just as much force, oblivious to the damage he'd caused. His frantic gaze scanned the room, then landed on me. "Hades! We need to talk."

"Little busy," I snapped.

Then I saw his face.

Poseidon looked like he'd aged a century since the last time I'd seen him. His skin had turned a sickly shade of gray. Tufts of his blond hair spiked out in a thousand different directions, and despair glittered his eyes. A sense of dread filled my gut.

I pulled him into the kitchen and closed the door behind us. For what felt like the thousandth time today I found myself asking, "What happened?"

Only this time I was afraid of the answer.

Chapter XXXIX

Aphrodite

I DIDN'T KNOW how long I'd been unconscious when Persephone found me, but I could tell she was worried.

"I need your help. Hades isn't answering me, and I'm in trouble." Persephone explained the situation with Triton, and I frowned. The kid shouldn't be able to overextend himself. Persephone was weird, because she had worshipers, but in most cases, power is a matter of having it or not. You can't work yourself into a deficit, no matter how motivated you are.

Unless he had worshipers.

No, Poseidon had been too careful. No one but Persephone had even known he had a son until she spilled the beans.

She looked around my dreamscape, her bedroom, and raised an eyebrow at me.

I opened my mouth to explain how much my life had changed in the last few weeks. Yes, it was weird. And part of me felt guilty for using her room as my dreamscape. But it was the closest thing to a home I'd ever known, and I had memories here with people who hadn't been charmed into hanging out with me.

"This is so nice of you," she said before I had a chance to explain. The worry on her face eased as she ran her fingers over her smooth wooden dresser. "For a while there I was worried I'd never see any of this again."

She dropped into the papasan chair and tucked her feet under her, looking so at home, and so much like she belonged here that the dreamscape wavered as I felt my place in it fading.

I shook my head, stabilizing the dreamscape, and summoned a chair for myself. "No problem. So about this kid—"

"I have a plan."

Alarm bells went off in my head when she told me what she was planning to do.

"Okay, wait, you—" A tugging sensation cut me off. "Persephone, I think I have to go."

She looked up, alarmed. "Wait! Will my idea help him? Will it work?"

"Yes, but he shouldn't—" I blinked, and the dreamscape changed around me. Now I stood in what looked like a board room. Over a dozen gods sat around a long conference table in black leather chairs.

"—need it," I finished. "What is this?" I crossed my legs and leaned back in my chair. I started to make a sarcastic comment about being knocked out, but then I saw everyone's faces.

There was no laughter or arrogance in Ares' face. He looked grim. Hephaestus stared down at his hands with a startling intensity, and Poseidon. Gods, Poseidon. What had I missed?

"I didn't get anyone to swear over, did I?" My eyes darted around to all the gods. "Where's Apollo? Did I—"

Hades shook his head. "Adonis knocked you out before you could do any damage. Zeus did get Apollo, but you had nothing to do with it."

I swallowed hard, fighting the compulsion to charm Ares and Hephaestus now that they were in front of me. It wasn't even possible to do unconscious. Charm was never real in dreamscapes, but that didn't seem to affect my body's desire to fulfill Zeus' orders. "If I didn't have anything to do with it, why did you bring me here?"

Demeter's and Hades' eyes flickered, like they wanted to look at each other but didn't dare, in case anyone noticed.

"We have to go ahead with our plan," Hades explained. "Now. Are you still willing to swear fealty?"

"Yeah," I said, shaken. "Just tell me who."

Chapter XL

Persephone

"TRITON?" I SHOOK his shoulder, worry turning my voice sharp.

He was bathed in sweat. Eyes fluttering open, he groaned. "S . . . top," he protested, pushing my hands away. "Hurts."

I stopped shaking him and stared at him wide-eyed in alarm. He didn't look so good. "What's wrong with you?"

He didn't reply, just groaned again and tried to roll over. I grabbed his shoulders to stop him. "Triton! Wake up."

"Where's my dad?" He tried to sit up and his face went ashen. Propping himself up on his arms, he sucked in deep breaths.

My pulse pounded in my throat. This was my fault. Triton hadn't come into his powers yet, and I'd been running him ragged. He'd overextended himself. I needed to help him.

"I don't know." I glanced at the water, which seemed higher than it had before, and the full helplessness of the situation hit me. I couldn't get him out of here. I couldn't go for help. I couldn't do anything. We were stuck here. "He'll find us."

"He's not here. He's never here." Triton's arms buckled, and he fell back onto the rocky floor of the cavern with a thud. "He's got more important things to do. A realm to run." Tears choked his voice. "He should have been here. He should have helped me."

I shushed him and brushed his hair off his face. "Your dad's looking for us. I know he is."

"It's all my fault. I shouldn't have left the circle. But I wanted to know what it was like out there." A sob broke through Triton's voice. "It hurt. It hurt so bad."

My hand froze on his forehead. Why was he talking in past tense? "Triton?"

He cried out, body going stiff, rigid.

"Triton!" There was no time to wait for Hades. I hadn't felt so much as a flicker of thought behind the wall he'd barricaded around his thoughts for over an hour.

Triton writhed and twisted, face contorted in pain. I looked back at the water, like it held some answers for me, but there was no help there. There was no help anywhere. Oh gods, this was either going to save him or kill him. I didn't know enough about how fealty worked. Would there be any holding back? I closed my eyes. *I swear—*

Persephone, stop!

Chapter XLI

Hades

PERSEPHONE, STOP! I yanked Persephone into my dreamscape with a thought. She stumbled into me.

"How am I here?" She looked around my dreamscape of the library wide-eyed.

I let the library fade into its usual indistinct swirls.

"Hades!" she demanded. "How am I here? I'm not sleeping."

My heart felt ready to beat right out of my chest. Had I not checked in on her right then . . . Had Aphrodite not told me what she had planned . . .

The thought made me cold. "Poseidon came to see me."

Irritation flashed in her green eyes. "What is he doing with you? Tell him to come here, now! Triton needs him."

I took a deep breath. "He can't find you."

"What do you mean he can't find us? We're in his realm! I should stick out like a sore thumb."

"Sit down, Persephone." I felt a flash of worry go through her at something in my voice. I hesitated, more rattled than I cared to admit. I didn't even know where to begin. "You're not in Poseidon's realm."

"What the hell are you talking about? Of course I'm in his realm. I've been playing little mermaid for weeks, so tell him to get his butt in gear and—"

An overwhelming sense of frustration and impatience tinged with panic washed through me. She fiddled with her necklace, and I closed my eyes. *Look.* I crossed the room, reaching for her. Her breath caught when my lips touched her forehead. I sifted through her thoughts. The last few weeks flashed across her mind as I dug through them. When I reached her escape from Zeus, I paused.

She'd stepped outside of her dream, leaving him in it. How had I missed that before? *You gave him control, Persephone.*

"No! I woke up."

I shook my head. *He just let you think you did. You never escaped. It was a distraction that kept you occupied and kept us busy looking for you.*

She stiffened. *I don't believe you.*

I can't lie.

"This is a trick!" Persephone shouted. She sprang out of her chair, fists clenched to her sides. You're not you at all! Zeus is messing with me again, he—

"I'm Hades, no tricks, no deception." I held my hands out to her in a placating gesture. "I know this is hard, but—"

"I would *know* if I were dreaming," she argued, green eyes flashing with fury and fear.

I let out a deep breath. "You did. Remember? I'm the one who convinced you it was real. I'm sorry."

"No!"

I stood, crossing the distance between us and tapping the air plant necklace that rested on her collarbone. "When you're with Triton, are you wearing that?"

She gave me an odd look at the change of subject. "Yes."

I reached into my pocket and pulled out her necklace, letting the rest of the room go blurry. "Look."

The necklace was in hyper focus, just like the two of us. Real objects in an otherwise intangible dream. Her hand went to the identical smear of a necklace dangling from her neck.

"It's a piece of your realm, Persephone. It's a conduit. Did you really think he would let you keep it?"

She reached out. Felt the pointy tips of the plant. The cool glass of the pomegranate. It was here. It was real. She couldn't deny it felt real.

The necklace around her neck wavered.

"Think. Even if he had let you keep it, you think you fell out of the sky into the ocean. I felt you land, Persephone. I felt you break. How come it didn't?" Any injury sustained while dreamwalking became real. Dreamwalking could be as much a weapon as a convenient communication method. But most gods kept their minds closed to intruders. Persephone had handed hers over to Zeus.

The blood drained from her face. "No," she whispered. I gripped her hand as the pieces fell into place in her mind with a horrifying click. She'd never escaped. She was still with Zeus.

"I'm sorry."

"But Triton. How is he—"

"Poseidon thinks he's with you. He can't feel him in his realm, and

Demeter would know if he crossed over to hers."

Images of Zeus sprang up in her mind. The things he'd done to her. "Zeus has Triton?" A vision of the child god moaning in agony flashed in my head. "That's what's wrong with him, isn't it? Zeus is doing something to him, and it's—" Her voice broke off with a sob. "Hades!"

"I know." I'd already determined to help him.

Iron glinted in her eyes. "How do I wake up?"

I hesitated. "It doesn't have to be you. I could—"

"I know all about your plan." She kissed my cheek, sending along a tangle of images of Aphrodite detailing my plan, and offering an out. A surge of anger swelled within me, but it was lost in the general storm of the emotion.

Every single thing that had happened since he'd taken her had been infuriating. Every fiber of my being was already saturated with rage.

And fear.

"You're not strong enough to go against Zeus."

She followed my line of thought, saw all the gods waiting for my word so they could swear fealty.

"So make me stronger." She touched her forehead to mine. "I love you. But I'm not worth breaking the world for."

"You are to me." I drew her into my arms and kissed her. My mind flitted to Demeter's plan, and I let out a deep breath, shielding my thoughts.

She would never forgive me. But she would be alive. "I'll try to filter it so the powers don't burn through you. It won't be enough to kill Zeus, but it may be enough to escape. Find the kid, then come back to me."

"But what about—"

"You aren't his only child. Let the others handle this. Once you find us, you can transfer the power to whomever you want. Ares is always itching for a fight." I put a picture of Ares in her mind so she'd recognize him. "You don't have to be the one to do this. Just get out, and be safe."

She nodded. "Okay, I'm ready."

"This is going to hurt," I warned her.

She sighed. "What else is new?"

Chapter XLII

Aphrodite

I BREATHED A sigh of relief when Hades reappeared in the board-room. Finally!

"Now," he commanded.

"This isn't going to work," Athena objected. "I understand why you'd want to filter the power and save her, but you must know it won't be enough."

I rolled my eyes. "Nothing is certain until you try, right? Zeus won't be expecting this, so maybe that's enough of an advantage." I smiled at Hades. "I swear fealty to Persephone." With a thought, I pushed as much of my power to her as I could and still live through it.

Athena sighed. "Fine. But if it doesn't work, you have to—"

"I know, Athena," Hades snapped. "Are you in, or would you rather try to fight Zeus by yourself?"

She pursed her lips. "I swear fealty to Persephone."

Ares bowed his head and closed his eyes, the words of fealty leaving his lips in a whisper. His voice was joined by Hephaestus' gruff utterance. Then Artemis' breathy announcement. Soon the room was ringing with the oath. The hair on my arms stood on end at the power flowing from this room. All directed to one little goddess.

Please let this work, I thought.

But I knew Athena was right. With Hades filtering the power, it would never be enough. Would he realize that before it was too late? Would he be willing to sacrifice Persephone to save us all? I had my doubts.

Chapter XLIII

Persephone

THE SUN SPARKLED through the glass ceiling. I was on a big white fluffy bed. When I noticed the thick shield surrounding the room, I closed my eyes. Shields. How had I been stupid enough to believe I'd escaped?

I gave myself a second to take inventory, amazed that after all I'd been through I was still in one piece. Even my clothes looked as clean and new as the day I'd bought them. *Just like when I woke up in the Underworld.*

I tried to get up but was jerked to a stop. Twisting to see behind me, I stared in disbelief at the handcuffs that bound my hands to the bedrail. Had I spent a single minute conscious since Zeus knocked me out in the park? Or were the handcuffs a new addition to Zeus' security measures?

I think it was the handcuffs that did it. A wave of fury washed through me so strong I felt Hades respond to it with surprise.

All this time. *All this time* I'd thought I was free, and I'd been bound to a bed with fricken handcuffs? I'd been helpless, and I was over being helpless. I thought over the last year. Pirithous grabbing my arm and trying to take me out of the flower shop. Boreas dragging me through the snow. Melissa hunched over with an icicle in her chest. Rachel's dead body in a crumbled heap outside my school. Aphrodite bound to obey Zeus' every word. Thanatos' eyes, wide with charm. Months of torment from the Reapers. *Everything* that had happened in the last year was because of Zeus. All the pain—oh, who was I kidding?—all the agony. All the frustration and hurt and fear. The paralyzing fear. It had been him. It had all been him.

I thought of the things I'd done that I didn't really remember. Each kiss he'd charmed from me under the guise of Joel. Zeus trying to use me to charm Hades, the torture, the lightning, the dreams, and Triton's face twisted in a grimace of agony. My *mom!* It was a never-ending litany of wrongs, and I was *done*.

"You're awake." Zeus' soft exclamation of surprise from the doorway had me jerking up, rigid with rage.

The handcuffs shattered, and I was off the bed and across the room in an instant. I tore through the shield like it wasn't there and knocked him off his feet, landing on top of him with enough force to knock the breath from my body.

"Where is Triton?" I didn't consider the possibility that Zeus pretended to be Triton in the dreamscape. Zeus was good, but he still couldn't lie. He'd called Poseidon his father, spoken of a million things that were only true for the prepubescent deity. Triton had been in my head, which meant he was here somewhere.

Zeus laughed. "What is this? I always figured you were feisty, but—"

My fist met his face with a satisfying crunch. The powers of over a dozen deities were at my disposal, but I ignored them, too blind with rage to want to do much more than hit something. So I did. I hit him over and over again, unable to stop myself. Zeus' face lost its amused expression. He reached up and blocked my next hit, hands wrapping around my wrists with a painful jolt of electricity.

I broke his grip and lashed out with a wave of power, throwing up a shield and inverting it around him, pinning him to the ground. "Where is he?"

"Neat trick. Thanks for showing it to me. It came in handy against your friends."

I narrowed my eyes at him and wrapped a hand around his throat, breaking my own shield. Hades' powers came to me unbidden. Black energy spread from my hands, turning Zeus' veins black.

"Okay, that's enough." Zeus threw up a shield, binding me against him, then rolled over on top of me, hipbones digging painfully into my flesh. "I may not be able to kill you." His breath was hot in my ear. "But that doesn't mean I can't make you scream."

Electricity coursed from him to me, and I arched my back, crying out in pain. His hands wrapped around my neck. Straddling me, he looked straight in my eyes. "You can still end this." He wasn't talking to me. "You know what I want. And I'm willing to do *anything* to get it."

Oh Gods, the lightning hadn't stopped. It flowed from his hands around my neck, down my spine to every nerve ending. My vision wavered. Lifting a hand, I tried to push him off me, but he moved one hand off my neck and pinned my arms above my head. I couldn't seem to call on any power while his coursed through me. He'd pinned me so tight I couldn't move my arms or legs. His face was inches from mine. Zeus' attention was on my hands as he struggled to keep them together. Lifting my head, I clamped my teeth into the skin of his neck, tearing them free when he let out a startled yelp.

Zeus swore and knocked my head into the floor with enough force to plant stars in my vision. "You stupid bitch!" He wrapped his hands around my throat. I pushed at them weakly, but his grip was iron tight.

"Where?" I gasped, drawing on as much power as I could.

"Dead, all right? I killed him."

My mind went blank with shock. I stopped struggling. Went limp beneath him.

Zeus' hands loosened a fraction. "A couple days before I captured you." He smirked. "Stupid kid didn't last an entire hour."

Days before Zeus captured me? "How? I was just with him!"

"He gave me everything, his power, access to his realm, thoughts, memories, dreamscapes, everything. Everything he was is up here." Zeus tapped his head. "I drained it all before I sent his empty shell of a soul to the Underworld."

I felt a start of surprise from Hades and caught a glimpse of a mental image. Triton in the throne room, face blank with shock before Cassandra whisked him away.

He was dead. He was really dead. I thought of his smile. His voice cracking, face turning bright red with embarrassment.

"It's all my fault. I shouldn't have left the circle. But I wanted to know what it was like out there." A sob broke through Triton's voice. "It hurt. It hurt so bad."

"You bastard!" I shrieked, lashing out with a wave of crackling energy encased in flame. "He was just a kid!"

Zeus deflected the blow, but his face tightened with pain. "You'll be joining him soon enough."

"I can't swear fealty to you! My promise—"

"To never act with intent of harming Hades?" Zeus laughed and drew his hand back. "Kind of depends on you being sane enough to understand intent." With that he slammed his fist into my gut, releasing wave after wave of lightning.

Chapter XLIV

Persephone

"PERSEPHONE . . ."

Stirring, my eyes fluttered open. "What?" I looked around, confused at finding myself curled up on the grass beneath a weeping willow.

Mom sat against the trunk, fingers combing through my hair. "Wake up, sweetie."

"How did I get here?" I sat up, looking around the picturesque landscape. Flowers bloomed everywhere. The sun shone bright in the sky, filtering through the green leaves of the weeping willow. Its trunk was just a little wider than Mom. That bugged me for some reason I couldn't put my finger on.

"You're dreaming, sweetheart."

Of course I was. A fresh wave of pain tore through me. I doubled over, gasping in agony. "Mom, it hurts."

She shushed me, voice soothing. "You're going to be okay."

"How can you say that?" I asked as another wave of pain washed over me.

"Because I know it's true. I am so sorry. I never wanted you to have this life. To make these decisions." She studied me, tears brimming in her eyes. "You were so small. Just this warm little bundle cuddled in my arms and now . . ." She swept her arm up and down over me. "You're all grown up." She wrapped her arms around me in a hug, and I leaned against her, taking some small measure of comfort despite the searing pain.

"Mom, I can't win."

"You have enough power to win, if you use it all."

"Hades is filtering—"

"Ask him to stop."

"I'll die." I moved away from her. I wanted to move her away from the tree. Something about it bothered me.

"Not because of that. You're about to come into your powers."

"How?"

She smiled. "I know a way, that's all. Come here." She reached out for me, but I jerked away.

"You're not telling me something."

"You're going to be fine."

"No. Mom, no more secrets. You owe me."

To my surprise, tears filled her eyes. "Will you trust me? Just this one last time. I promise, after this there will be no more secrets."

"Mom . . . "

She shook her head and brushed the tears out of her eyes. "I'm just being over emotional. Now, we'd best hurry. If Zeus figures out what I'm doing, he'll go underground, and you'll spend your whole life wondering when he's going to come at you again."

I nodded, though I still felt uncertain. But I couldn't focus because I was still trying to figure out what was bothering me about that damn willow tree. It's hard to pay attention in dreams, but it's foolish to overlook a symbol. Everything has meaning.

She knelt before me. "I swear fealty—"

"Mom," I flushed and forgot the tree in my embarrassment. "You don't have to do that. I can't take your power—"

She hushed me and wrapped a hand around my wrist. "I'm giving you your best chance." She narrowed her eyes at me and gave me her "don't argue" look. Then softer, she said, "Your very best chance. I love you darling."

Her power slammed into me like a boulder crashing down from the sky. I stumbled back, but her grip tightened on me like an iron vise.

Why can't we plant a weeping willow? I'd asked.

"Mom! What are you doing? It's too much!" But she wouldn't let me go. Then all at once it was gone. Not her power, but that feeling of being bombarded, overwhelmed. Pain I hadn't even realized I was feeling was gone. It was like something snapped into place within me. I felt full, complete. Alive.

Never plant a willow tree, she'd replied.

She smiled at me, looking frail and vulnerable. Smaller somehow. As I stared at her, she changed. Her hair and eyes brightened, all the little details that made up her appearance suddenly became more obvious, hyper-realistic.

Because as soon as the trunk grows wide enough—

"No," I whimpered. "Mom, no."

It becomes your coffin.

I was looking at her soul.

"I love you *so* much," she whispered. Then she was gone.

I fell to the ground as her dreamscape faded around me. "No," I whispered, broken. Tears chased each other down my cheeks, but I wasn't given more than a second to mourn before I felt the power of all the other gods slam into me, unfiltered from Hades. I felt them tethered to me, alive. It wasn't fair.

Your very best chance. Her voice whispered through my memory.

Chapter XLV

Hades

PERSEPHONE SAT at the base of the weeping willow, sobbing.

"I'm sorry," I whispered.

She sprang to her feet at the sound of my voice, whirling on me. "Bring her back!"

"I'm so sorry." My voice was hoarse with grief. "I can't."

"I *gave* you Thanatos' power! Use it!"

I shook my head. She was asking the impossible and she knew it.

Rage flashed in her eyes, and I felt her pull upon the power of the other gods. Maybe she even tried to use it on me, but her oath to never hurt me held.

"I wasn't asking. Bring her *back!*"

"I *can't*, Persephone." I moved forward, arms encircling her, and she broke, folding into me. "I can't," I whispered. "I'm so sorry, I can't."

She drew back. "You knew she was going to do that?"

She knew. I didn't need to answer but did anyway. "It was the only way to trigger you coming into your powers early. Persephone, it was your only chance."

It was hard to watch her struggle with that. I was the *only* person in her life who had never once misled her. And now that was gone, along with her mother. "I offered my plan as an alternative, but she didn't want to risk the rest of the world any more than you did."

"What good is the rest of the world without her in it?" Her eyes glittered. "It needs her. *I* need her."

But Persephone didn't need Demeter. She hadn't for a long time. And the world only needed Demeter's power, which now resided in Persephone. But now wasn't the time to lay the burden of the planet at her feet. Persephone had reached the last line of her defense. Questions. You can ask almost anything without lying.

There's a reason there are seven stages of grief. It takes time for the mind to process tragedy. Grief, true grief, needs the cushion of denial and anger and blame to cope.

"Tell me I'm overreacting," she begged. "Tell me I'll see her in the Underworld every day, and that everything is going to be—"

I pulled her back to me, letting her sob into my shoulder. She'd seen Demeter's soul vanish. Persephone knew what that meant. Demeter had given her everything, mind, body, and soul. There was nothing left of her. It wouldn't have worked otherwise.

"I'm sorry," I said again. Apologies were all I had left to offer. "I'm so sorry."

Her thoughts went in endless circles while she tried to accept what had just happened. There was a glimmer of rationality, and then her mind latched on to someone she could feel angry at. Someone she could blame.

Zeus.

Chapter XLVI

Persephone

THE DREAMSCAPE faded around me as I regained consciousness. I found Zeus still on top of me, still hitting me with wave after wave of lightning. It had probably only been seconds since I'd lost consciousness, but it felt like a lifetime.

I kept my eyes closed, concentrating on the power he kept pulsing through me. A ghost of a plan passed on from my mother rooted in my mind. Gathering a small shield around my hand, I channeled the power to it—my power, the power of the other gods, and his own lightning. When the shield stretched to the breaking point, my eyes flew open.

Zeus jerked back in surprise, but I was ready. I brought my hand up, slamming it into him, then through him as I pulled on Thanatos' power to influence souls. My hand turned white as it wrapped around Zeus' soul.

Zeus' eyes widened as he realized I had the upper hand. I didn't have to overpower him. I didn't have to be stronger than he was. All I had to do was squeeze. My fist clenched and he sputtered in shock.

"No, no, don't! I'll swear fealty. I'll swear! I'll give you every drop of my power. Just leave me enough to live."

A smile curved on my lips, and I allowed myself one second to relish the feeling of being strong, powerful, in control. For once, I wasn't the one quaking in fear. I loosened my grip. "Better get on with it then."

Zeus' mouth twisted in a snarl. "Oh, I'll swear all right." He chuckled. "I swear fealty."

With that oath, his power slammed into me. Unprepared, I lost my grip and lurched backward. He pressed one hand to my chest, just above my heart, and let loose a torrent of power, bright and blinding like the sun, while his other hand wrapped around my throat. Again.

Gods, what was it with Zeus and chokeholds? I felt my flesh smoldering beneath his touch until my vocal cords withered and snapped under the pressure.

Give me teleportation rights, quick! Hades demanded.

Do what? I had no idea how to do what he was talking about.

Hades swore. I had the mental impression of being shoved aside. It reminded me of when I took too long to do something on the computer, and Melissa would snatch the keyboard and start typing away. Only in my head.

A pulse of power passed from me to Hades, followed by a long string of numbers I didn't understand.

"You gotta get better with your wording, sweetheart," Zeus sneered. "I gave you all *my* power. This is someone else's."

His fist drew back again. Words. He'd sworn fealty. I could order him to stop, but my scorched vocal cords couldn't form words.

Hades' hand shot out, intercepting Zeus' fist. "That," he grunted, lifting Zeus from me and throwing him against a wall, "is the *last* time you touch my wife." His free hand smashed into Zeus' face, and black veins spread across his skin.

Zeus let out an enraged roar, and the two exchanged blows, but it was obvious Hades had the upper hand. I gasped as my healing kicked in. Hades' head jerked toward me at the sound, and Zeus surged forward, a flash of power emitting from his right hand in a bright blaze. Something shimmered in his left, something metal. Light fractured around it.

Voice restored, I shouted, "Stop!" Quick as a thought, I teleported in front of Hades. I didn't know what that thing was in his left hand, but every instinct screamed to me that it was dangerous.

Zeus froze, mid-slash. Shoving him into the wall, I gritted my teeth against the pain of the spike slicing into my arm.

I took his soul in my hand, and his eyes widened in shock. "I surrender."

It didn't matter. "Then tell me the absolute truth. No hedging, no double speak. What will you do now you're sworn to me? Now that you've surrendered?"

Zeus' jaw tightened. "Plot every minute of the rest of my existence to put an end to you and *take* my powers back, you miserable little bitch." He smiled. "I won't have to wait long."

"Yeah, I thought so."

"Doesn't matter. You're not going to kill me. You don't have it in you." His lips twisted in a smirk. "I know you. I've seen everything that goes on in that empty head of yours. You're not strong enough."

It didn't take strength to kill someone. It took fear. Fear and the knowledge he would come back, that nothing and no one in my life would be safe so long as he walked the earth. I finally understood why Hades kept saying I was brave, kept claiming I was strong. He'd misinterpreted my naiveté for bravado.

His eyes turned cunning. "You're different than the rest of us. And that's okay. You're . . . you're . . . "

"A novelty?" I supplied, quoting back his earlier words.

"More than that. So much more. You don't want to do this. You don't want to be like us. You're different."

I was. And maybe I always would be. But this wasn't just about what I wanted. I wouldn't be the only in danger if I let him go. The other gods had given me everything they had so I would end this. Mom had died for this. Her realm was my responsibility now, as much as the Underworld. Maybe this would make me a monster, but everyone has to grow up sometime.

I looked Zeus straight in the eye. "Drop dead."

The spike clattered to the floor, and the rest of Zeus' power slammed into me. Hades snatched the spike, swearing as recognition dawned in his eyes.

I stumbled backward, clutching at my arm. The pain from the scratch lanced up to my elbow, spreading like wildfire. Hades steadied me, and I felt a pulse of power pass through me.

My heart stopped beating. I gasped, sinking to my knees. Hades held onto me, lowering me to the floor. He grabbed my arm just above the elbow. "Where does it hurt?" When I didn't answer right away, he shouted the question over and over again in my face, panic evident in his eyes.

"Elbow." Though the pain was creeping higher.

"Okay." He nodded like he'd just made some decision. "Okay, it'll grow back."

Grow back? What the hell was he talking about, grow back?

I followed his train of thought and shook my head, trying desperately to scramble out of his iron grip. *No, stop!*

His hand tightened around my upper arm like a vise. Agony spread from his fingers, and my screams echoed from the rafters. Hades' other hand went to my forehead, and then blissful darkness washed over me.

Chapter XLVII

Hades

I TELEPORTED TO Demeter's backyard, then to the throne room in the Underworld. Persephone hung limp in my arms, face drained of all color. Her dress saturated with blood.

"Take her!" I demanded to a startled Charon. He opened his mouth, no doubt about to ask what happened. I didn't give him the chance. Depositing Persephone into his arms, I teleported back to Zeus' palace, grabbed the Olympian Dagger, and teleported to Demeter's living room.

There were gasps and exclamations of surprise from the gods, and for a second I wondered what *I* must look like. I was no doubt covered in her blood. But before they could bombard me with questions, I grabbed Hephaestus by the shirt collar and yanked him toward me. Brandishing the Olympian Steele, I held it to his throat, careful not to so much as scratch his skin.

"You swore there were none left!" I shouted. I didn't need to be this rattled, this emotional, this angry, not in this room with these gods, but there was no help for it.

Hephaestus blanched. "I . . . But . . . there's no way—"

"You swore you'd melted down the very last of these abominations and taken their power into yourself. You *swore!*" I shook him like a rag doll.

Long ago, Hephaestus discovered some way to forge metal that could take down any god. The metal was infused with power that could kill in a matter of heartbeats. These weapons weren't picky. A simple scratch or nick, anything that drew blood, and you were done for unless you acted fast.

"I did!"

"Then how the hell did Zeus have *this?*" Please gods, let me have been fast enough. Let her wake up. I'd done everything, hadn't I? Stopping her heart stopped her circulation, and then I removed the infected

Katlin Bevis

area. She'd healed. That had to be a good sign, right? Crippling uncertainty gripped me like a vise. I wasn't used to feeling uncertain. Once I told Persephone I'd never felt fear before I'd met her.

Now I was making up for lost time.

"I don't know! But it's not mine! I didn't make this one, I swear."

The words took a minute to sink in. If Hephaestus didn't make this, then who did?

Luckily I knew who to ask.

Releasing Hephaestus so fast he stumbled backward, I was suddenly aware of everyone else in the room. The gods all had their eyes fixated on the Olympian Dagger. I clutched death in the palm of my hand.

No one fears death more than immortals. Humans adjust to their lot in life little bits at a time. They're introduced to the concept with goldfish, then move up to puppies, ancient relatives and reckless friends, each victim closer to them than the last. Death follows them through life, making itself known. Numbing them bit by bit until there is nothing left in them but resignation. We had no such preparation. We were never meant to die.

"Is she dead?" Melissa's shaky question shattered the silence of the room. It swelled and exploded into a million questions coming so fast and loud they blended together in an indistinct cacophony of chaos.

"Did she kill Zeus?"

"— our power!"

"—that weapon!"

"—break fealty."

"—Olympian Steele! We need to—"

"She's alive." *Please stay that way.* "He's dead. And I'm going back to the Underworld."

"You swore she would break the bonds of fealty." Athena's eyes glittered with impatience.

My hand itched to slash the dagger across her throat. Persephone had gone through hell, sheer hell, while Athena sat on Demeter's couch.

"Where's my son?" Poseidon's question made me wince. I'd forgotten about Triton.

I didn't say anything, didn't have to. Poseidon read the answer on my face. His knees buckled under him, face going blank with shock.

"I'm sorry," I managed. And I was, for the kid.

"I didn't deserve him." Poseidon's voice was raw.

No one argued. There are no shades of gray to gods. Without the ability to lie and make justifications, it's difficult *not* to have a strong sense of justice. Poseidon was worse than most of us, but that any of us were able to look in the mirror every morning after the things we'd done was no small miracle.

None of us deserved to be happy, and we knew it. We didn't deserve to have anything or anyone good in our lives. Gods, they'd known it. The Titans knew the abominations we would become. The horrific deeds we would commit. All the ways we would go on to abuse our creations. They'd tried to end our existence, to stop us, and in return we orchestrated their murder. We'd killed our parents. And then we created a species in our image, acting surprised when they spent every waking moment improving upon their methods of murder and mass destruction. We did that. We made them sadistic and twisted and broken. We were gods. Every bad thing that had *ever* happened lay at our feet. There was no one else to blame.

Every good thing, every happy moment filled me with dread because we didn't deserve it. I'd spent my whole life with baited breath waiting for the day I'd have to answer for what I'd done. Zeus, Hera, Hestia, Demeter, Poseidon, they'd all paid the price for their sins. I was the only one left.

The thought had a prophetic ring to it, and my thoughts leapt to Persephone, unconscious and soaked in her own blood. *Please, please don't let her be my price.*

I must have teleported. Suddenly I was in the Underworld, in Persephone's room, standing beside her. She lay on top of the covers, arms folded over a bouquet of flowers on her chest like she was laid out in a casket. I made a strangled sound at the sight, startling Cassandra who was curled up in a papasan chair by Persephone's bed.

"Hades!" She put a hand to her chest, like she could feel her heart beating faster in fear. Ridiculous, of course. Souls are heartless creatures. "Hypnos said it would help. The flowers I mean. Something about the energy?" She motioned around the room, and I noticed flowerpots and vases filled with a variety of plant life for the first time. "Hades, what happened? Why isn't she waking up?"

"Like you don't know."

Cassandra flinched at my voice. "I'll um . . . just . . ." She climbed out of the chair and edged toward the door. "I'll check on you in a bit."

The door closed with a click. I sank onto the bed, fumbling for Persephone's hand and knocking aside the flowers. Her hands were cold. I'd broken her. I'd always known I would.

"Please," I whispered, touching my forehead to hers. "Wake up." Why was she so cold? I shifted my grip on her hand and touched two fingers to her wrist.

No pulse.

"Oh." Well, now I felt really stupid. I touched my lips to hers, sending a ping of power through her to start her heart and repair the damage done in its absence. She gasped, eyes fluttering open.

It was a fairy tale moment. My kiss bringing her back to life. Or it would have been had it not been my stupidity that kept her under in the first place. *Of course* she couldn't regain consciousness until I restored her heartbeat.

"Hades," she whispered. A smile touched her lips, and nothing else mattered.

Chapter XLVIII

Aphrodite

I OPENED MY EYES in a panic. Were they stupid? How could they let me wake up? Zeus ordered me to charm them into swearing fealty. That wasn't going to go away unless . . .

Unless . . .

Blinking, I took in my surroundings. I lay on Demeter's white couch in her cheerful living room with dozens of gods milling around, looking distressed. Craning my neck, I sought out Ares. His grin sent a rush of relief coursing through me. No overwhelming desire to charm him. Zeus must be dead.

I was free.

"Good nap?" Melissa's sarcastic voice was music to my ears.

"It worked?" I demanded, swinging my legs off the couch and turning to face her.

"More or less. Zeus is dead, but so are Demeter and Triton. Persephone is MIA, and Hades seemed . . ." Melissa chewed her bottom lip. "Well . . . "

"Worried?"

"Unhinged." She looked down. "He was also covered in blood."

I raised an eyebrow and was about to comment when Persephone and Hades appeared in the middle of the living room. "Speak of the devil."

Melissa's eyebrows drew together in confusion, and I motioned behind her. She turned and gasped when she saw Persephone. Everyone else was closer, but Melissa shoved through them to reach Persephone first and yanked her into an embrace.

I studied Persephone, half afraid she would be different. With everything she'd been through, she should have been marked by some kind of a physical change. But she looked exactly the same. Leaning into Hades, she didn't seem nearly happy enough to finally be done with this whole horrible situation. But in a way, the horror of Zeus' capture was only just starting. Soon she'd have to deal with the fallout of her victory. Of Demeter's death. Her eyes were filled with the weight of that sadness and fatigue.

Which was understandable given the circumstances.

Persephone clung to Melissa for a moment then pulled away. Hades stood behind her, hand drifting from her shoulder, to the small of her back, to her hand. He didn't seem to be able to stop touching her. Happiness would be out of place here, but he looked like the worry and stress had melted away from him.

"It's nice to see you in person." Athena smiled at Persephone and held out her hand.

Persephone's eyes narrowed. "You're the one who wanted me to die."

Athena's smile froze on her face. "It's nothing personal—"

"Right." Persephone grabbed Athena's hand and slammed Athena's power back into her, breaking the bond of fealty. "Nothing personal."

Athena stumbled backward, gasping for breath.

I smiled. It was about time Persephone grew a backbone. I watched Athena, speculating on how it must feel to have made such a powerful enemy. Persephone was kind of a big deal now. Since Triton had sworn to Zeus, and he had sworn to Persephone, she had access to every realm in creation, and the power to pretty much blow up every god in this room.

"Aphrodite!" To my surprise, Persephone pulled me into a hug. She drew back, locking gazes with me, and what I saw there brought tears to my eyes. Persephone understood.

We'd both been manipulated and abused by Zeus, and we'd both fought to overcome him in the end. Sure, her success had been more dramatic, but I'd played a part. And that was a pretty big deal for someone who'd been programmed to be loyal to Zeus.

"This is yours." She pushed my power back into me, and I held up a hand before she broke the bond of fealty.

"Don't. Mine wasn't conditional. After everything I did to you, it's the least I can do for you."

She looked surprised but didn't argue. "If you ever change your mind—"

"I won't." Zeus may be dead, but I still had to obey everyone in his bloodline who outranked me. That left only Persephone. I wanted my loyalty and my obedience to be my choice, not something forced upon me.

She nodded, then moved on to the rest of the gods, restoring power and breaking fealty bonds, not pausing until she came to Poseidon. "I'm so sorry," she whispered, almost too low for me to hear. "He was incredible. It isn't right that he—" Tears overwhelmed her voice.

Poseidon clutched her hands in his, looking devastated. "Thank you for being there for him." His voice was gruff. "For making his last memories better than what Zeus left him with." He cleared his throat. "Can you restore his soul?"

She nodded. "Not enough to bring him back to life, but I should be able to put him back together. He'll be able to dreamwalk, so you'll see him again."

Well, that was enough reunion crap for me. I reached down and grabbed my purse, reaching for my sunglasses and car keys.

"Where are you going?" Melissa asked.

"Are you kidding? I'm out of here. I was thinking of heading back to Florida. What can I say? I miss the beach." I looked at Melissa for a minute, knowing the answer before I asked and hating it. "Want to come? I could charm your teachers for you."

Melissa shook her head. "I'm staying here, but maybe I'll visit over spring break."

"Suit yourself." I slid on my sunglasses.

"I think you're forgetting something," Melissa said.

"Hmm?"

She reached out and snatched the keys from my hands. "Those are my car keys."

"Need a ride?" Ares asked, flashing me a grin.

I glanced between him, Adonis, and Hephaestus, all suddenly holding car keys.

Choices, choices. I took a moment to relish the freedom to make my own decisions. A grin broke out on my face. Choices were fun and all, but why pick one when you can have all three?

"Road trip?" I suggested.

Chapter XLIX

Hades

SHE'D WOKEN UP screaming again.

But it hadn't taken long for her to return to sleep. I leaned against the headboard, one hand rhythmically stroking her hair. Power flowed through my fingertips, keeping her nightmares at bay.

I could deal with nightmares. And really, after everything she'd been through, if sleepless nights were the only noticeable change, we were lucky. She had her moments during the day—if something reminded her of her mother, or whenever she saw Triton in a crowd of souls—but for the most part she was coping well. She was stronger than I'd ever given her credit for. I could handle emotional breakdowns.

What I couldn't handle, what set my heart beating in rage, was the fear in her eyes when she woke from her nightmares and saw me. The second when she wasn't sure whether I was myself, or Zeus in disguise.

But I'd discovered a nice outlet for my anger. When I was certain she wouldn't wake again, I shifted the covers to the side, climbed out of bed, and teleported to the deepest, darkest dimension of Tartarus.

A white room with a single metal chair.

"Back again?" Zeus sounded amused. He looked comfortable, no small accomplishment given that he was strapped to the chair and only half-healed from the Prometheus treatment. I didn't always keep him in here of course. There was an entire realm full of all the tortures Zeus had inflicted on us over the millennia.

I summoned all the equipment I'd need. Knives today. Perhaps a table. I'd wanted to torch his soul the moment it entered the Underworld, but I had questions that needed answers. The missing demigods were not in the Underworld. We needed to locate them and find out how he'd gotten ahold of Olympian Steele.

Plus, torturing Zeus was kind of fun.

"So, how's the wife?"

I stiffened, but said nothing.

Zeus grinned. "I'm sure she's adjusting well. She's quite the trooper. Fastest recovery times I've ever seen. Did I tell you about the time I ripped out one of her lungs?" He laughed. "You should have seen her flopping around like—"

My fist hit his face with a satisfying crunch.

"Enjoy that?" Blood and spittle drooled from Zeus' mouth. Tartaran souls could bleed, otherwise where would the fun be?

"A little."

He smirked. "I wonder about you sometimes, Hades. You've got that hot piece of ass warming your bed, and instead of enjoying it, you're here beating the daylights out of me. Unless . . ." He paused dramatically. "You've figured it out."

I didn't rise to the bait. Instead I laid the knives out on the table.

Zeus waited for me to ask, but when it became clear I wasn't going to, he continued on as if I'd spoken. "You know she doesn't love you as much as you love her, right? I've been in her head. There's not much going on up there, but when she thinks of you there's always a caveat."

"Where are the demigods?" I examined one of the knives in the light.

"You should have seen her face when she thought I was you. She was so happy, so certain you had come to rescue her." He smiled. "She pressed that hot little body against me." He studied my face for a long moment as if calculating how far he could push me before I snapped. "It's been quite some time since I've been kissed like that. She's got so much . . . spirit. I took great pleasure in watching that spirit drain out of her while I hacked her to pieces."

Persephone's face flashed into my mind, eyes wide with fear. Screw the demigods. I summoned the Olympian Steele. "There's something I've wondered for quite some time."

Zeus' grin faltered. "You won't do anything permanent. You need me. You want to know where I got that Steele, and you want to know about those demigods."

"What would happen if I used this on a soul?" I approached Zeus.

"You need me."

"No, I don't." Zeus was never going to tell me what I wanted to know. He knew it was the only thing keeping his soul intact. Maybe she would sleep better if I torched his soul. I touched the Steele to his skin.

"I didn't touch the demigods." Zeus' eyes darted from the Steele to me. I applied more pressure.

"Then I really don't need you."

"Yes, you do. You need me more than ever. You think you saved the world by killing me, but you've doomed it. What's coming is worse. And Hades—" he inclined his head to the Steele "—they're armed."

I considered for a moment.

"You need me," Zeus insisted. "You want to be prepared for what's to come."

If Zeus wasn't responsible for the demigods, then who was?

Did it matter?

I was probably going to regret this. But I was done. I was done being manipulated by Zeus.

"You need me." He locked eyes with me. "You know you do."

"Like hell."

I WIPED THE BLOOD from my hands as I exited the torture chamber. In the blink of an eye I was in my restroom in fresh clothes reaching for a washcloth.

"Can't sleep?"

I dropped the washcloth in the sink and turned to find Persephone standing behind me, bathed in light. "Sorry, didn't mean to wake you."

"I don't mind." She reached for the now pristine washcloth I held in my left hand, the movement sending one of the thin straps of her white nightgown slipping down her arm. "Are you okay? I thought I saw—"

"I'm fine." I dropped the washcloth in the sink.

Persephone's green eyes searched my face and I smiled at the worry I found there. All she'd been through, and she was worried about me.

"Nothing to worry about." My fingers trailed over her smooth skin as I pushed the strap of her nightgown back into place. She tilted her head, leaning into my touch. Abandoning the strap I caressed her face, leaning down to touch my lips to hers.

"I love you," she whispered, arms twining around my neck.

I pulled her to me, wrapping my arms around her.

"I love you, too."

Chapter L

Persephone

TRITON'S FACE WAS completely blank. He sat on the bed, not seeming to notice when I came in. I took a deep breath. "I am so sorry for what happened to you."

He didn't blink. Didn't move.

I leaned down and kissed him on the forehead, releasing the bond of fealty he'd sworn to Zeus that I'd inherited and giving him back his memories, his thoughts, and his soul. There were parts of him I kept. I didn't have a choice in the matter; his powers wouldn't return to him now that he was dead. I'd give them to Poseidon next time I saw him.

The life returned to Triton's eyes, and I moved away from him and sat on a chair next to his bed.

"I know you," he said after a moment. He paused as if he were sorting through his memories. "Kind of."

"Kind of." I still didn't fully understand how Triton had been in my dreamscape after his death. Hades had tried to explain Zeus essentially just held on to Triton's soul and tossed him into a dreamscape of Poseidon's realm in case Zeus needed information from Triton later. When I stepped out of my dreamscape, Zeus saw the opportunity to throw me into Triton's, manipulating me into thinking I was waking up there, when in reality all I was doing was hopping from dreamscape to dreamscape.

Hades thought Zeus had a prophet telling him his plans, or at the very least a mole. He hadn't realized until the very end it was him. I'd surrendered my mind to Zeus, and Hades kept me informed of every step of the god's plans through our link. The only time I'd been out of Zeus' "earshot" was when I was in Hades' dreamscape, but that privacy only lasted until I was back in Triton's dreamscape, allowing Zeus to sit in on all our meetings right after they happened.

I'd stopped trying to wrap my head around the whole thing about ten minutes into Hades' lengthy explanation. All I needed to know was that Triton was down here without a part of his soul. That I could fix.

He glanced around the room. "So this is the Underworld?"

I nodded, not sure how he was going to take the news.

He raised his eyebrows. "Weird. I would have thought it was all underground and cave-like. Hey, can I meet Hades? Is he blue? You know, like that movie? Is his hair on fire? Can I meet Cerberus? Dad said he was the best dog. Oh, are there nymphs here . . . ?"

I smiled despite myself as Triton continued chattering. Yeah. He was going to be fine.

Later, in the living realm, I swung by my mom's flower shop to make sure Laurel, one of Mom's higher-ranking priestesses, had everything she needed.

"Are you sure you want me to run it?" she asked for what felt like the thousandth time.

"For now." Looking around the shop, I could almost see my mom at every corner. A smudge of dirt on her cheek from working on the nursery out back, talking on the phone with that unflappable patience. My eyes filled as I realized we'd never get back to that. Everything had been so normal before Pirithous had walked through these doors. I hadn't known what I had.

And now it was gone.

"You're going to be every bit as amazing as she was, I know it." Laurel smiled at me through a sheen of tears.

"She's going to be better." Melissa came down the stairs from where she'd been packing up the last of Aphrodite's things. "Hey, this came today." She picked up a stack of mail from the counter top. "I figured I'd bring it, and then we could go celebrate."

"Celebrate?" What could I possibly have to celebrate?

"Um, yeah, it's our birthday. Yay eighteen."

I blinked. I'd forgotten.

"And you sort of saved the day. And of course—" Melissa took one of the letters and handed it to me. It was from UGA. Confetti drawing decorated the envelope, and written in the corner in big red letters was "Your official acceptance letter."

"Kind of takes all the mystery out of opening it." I took the letter from her, and she held up another envelope, its twin.

"I know, right? But good news. Apparently we both got in."

The phone rang and Laurel answered it, disappearing into the back of the shop.

"What happened to Iowa?" I looked at Melissa. I knew she'd been accepted into the creative writing program there.

She waved a dismissive hand. "After everything you went through, please. My place is here. You need me now more than ever."

I looked at the envelope. It wasn't addressed to me, it was addressed to Kora. I'd gone by Kora my whole life, especially after Orpheus told the whole planet that Persephone was a goddess. This letter, the apartment above the shop, Melissa and I going to college together—it was all I'd wanted for so long. A return to normal life.

I dropped the envelope in the shredder.

Melissa yelped in surprise. "What are you doing?"

"I'm not Kora anymore." There was no going back to normal, and for the first time, I was okay with that. I wasn't human, but that didn't mean I had to be some evil, crazy goddess either. There was blood on my hands, but I hadn't enjoyed it. If after everything I'd gone through I was still connected enough to give a damn, then I was going to be just fine. "And you're not giving up your dreams for my sake."

"Don't you need me here?"

I shook my head. "Not as a priestess. You're my best friend. I can teleport, remember? I'll swing by to hang out, maybe cry on your shoulder a bit."

She gave me a hug. "Anytime." She pulled away from me and looked into my eyes. "Are you okay?"

"No." I shook my head, thinking of Hades, how he was willing to break the world for me. The way he'd held me together when my whole life seemed to shatter. The strength he saw in me I hadn't even known was there. I'd survived Pirithous. I'd survived Boreas. And I *destroyed* Zeus. I could handle grief. "But I will be."

Triton
A Short Story

"WHOA, LOOK AT this stuff!" I wriggled my tail to push through the narrow opening of the metal shipping container, wincing when the jagged metal scraped against my scales.

Shipwrecks didn't happen all that often, but shipping containers fell off boats all the time. I never got to leave The Circle to find them. Dad wouldn't let me. So when I heard that a shipping container settled on the upper shelf, I took off.

"Neat." Rhode's voice sounded way too dry for something so high pitched. The small dolphin didn't even *look* at the shipping container tilted along the sandy edge of the upper shelf. "Triton, as fascinating as this . . . collection you've got going is, people are starting to talk."

What people? Between the ocean and the islands, Dad's realm was chock full of "mythical" beings. But the thing about Cyclopes, Harpies, Sea Nymphs, or any of the others is that they're barely smarter than the regular fish in the sea. Barely. Anything with high reasoning skills had either been killed off or mixed with the humans eons ago. Dad kept the stragglers around because they were with it just enough to worship him.

"So you've said." Over and over again. "Keep watch." I pulled a conch shell from the kelp pouch that hung from my shoulder and blew it like a horn. The water inside the rusted shipping container poured past me into the sea. When it was completely dry inside, I stepped in.

My fin rippled and a tickle of power trickled across my tail like sea foam. Tiny bubbles of power pricked against my scales as they split into legs. As my feet touched down inside the slanted container I realized the tilt looked a lot more drastic from the inside.

"That doesn't hurt?" Rhode trilled.

I winced at the familiar question. She asked it every time I cursed her with sentience. The memories that came with basic sentience don't stick once my powers falter and mine faltered a *lot*. By rights, I shouldn't even be able to use them yet, but I wasn't exactly normal, even for a god.

"Nah. Just kind of tickles." Sometimes I got sick of answering the same questions over and over, but Rhode had a dry humor that was different from any of the other residents of The Circle. And in my boring world, anything different was good.

Besides, a little repetition was leagues better than being alone. I explored the shipping container. There wasn't a lot of room to walk around, maybe a foot in either direction because of all the boxes and stuff.

I ripped away the opaque plastic sheeting blocking my way to the boxes, but then ran into another problem. Some kind of a plastic strap, stronger than any rope I'd ever seen, held the boxes against the metal walls. "What is *this*?" I tugged at the plastic stuff, but it wouldn't break.

"Oh, a dingle-hopper of course," Rhode snarked behind me.

I scowled at the reference and tugged at the stuff for a few seconds longer before sawing away at it with the edge of my conch shell.

Finally the rope-like thing broke.

"YES!" I pulled down one of the boxes and ripped through the soaked and pulpy paper-like material it was made from and pulled out a bright, yellow rubber ducky. "Moby Duck! Ha!"

"Moby what?" Rhode nosed her way into the container, coming to a stop where the water ended.

"Okay, so like way in the early nineties, a *ton* of shipping containers went missing. Beach combers have been looking for these little rubber ducks," I squeezed the bath toy and gave a delighted laugh at the squeaky sound it made "for, like, ever! Oh man!"

I went on and on about the missing shipping containers even though I saw her eyes glaze over with boredom. I knew she'd tuned me out, but couldn't stop the words from pouring out of my mouth. Even the illusion of someone listening was too good to waste. I punched open another soggy box and pulled out more ducks. "I wish I could post about this!"

"Don't let your father hear you say that." Rhode clicked in disapproval.

She didn't have to tell me twice.

My divinely waterproof smart phone was the only thing that kept me sane! Dad had set it up somehow to where I could receive data, but not send it, which was kind of annoying, but I got it. People had never really stopped searching for The Circle. One slip up from me and all the creatures Dad saved by creating this shielded paradise could be—

Oh crud. "Rhode, what tide is it?"

"Half past Ebb," she chirped. "Why?"

I winced. "I'm late."

THIS ONE TIME, one of the Nereids that Dad gifted with enough higher reasoning to babysit, asked me to describe my father in three words for some random craft she'd seen on Pinterest. For some reason, we never finished. Maybe it was because the words I picked—busy, angry, and sad— didn't fit into her master plan to suck up to Dad enough to keep high-intelligence. I'd feel worse about ruining her plan if it actually would have made a difference. But Dad never would have gone for high-intelligence long term, anyway. Nereids reminded him too much of Mom.

Busy. Angry. Sad.

I tried to keep every piece of that puzzle in mind as Dad paced in front of his throne and tore into me for being late, but it wasn't easy.

"I am not made of time, Triton!" Dad railed, throwing his hands in the air. "I have a realm to run!" His voice echoed in hollow chamber. Water filled our underwater castle, tinting the algae and sand-colored spiraled columns blue. His voice shouldn't have been able to echo like that, what with the lack of walls and all, but the laws of physics didn't exactly apply within Dad's castle.

The inside of the castle acted as a neutral space and changed to meet the needs of those within it. Most of the time that meant variations in light, density, or oxygen levels for guests, but for Dad it meant the ability to echo. Like he wasn't loud enough already.

"Do you know what your mother sacrificed to even give you a *chance* like this?"

"Everything," I rasped, then cleared my throat. I hated him for throwing her at me almost as much as I hated myself for enjoying this conversation. He was talking to me. This wasn't a screen or an en-chanted dolphin or any other one sided connection. These were real words. And even though they hurt, I couldn't stop myself from soaking up the sensation.

"Everything!" The word met water like a heavy stone, shoving it away from my Dad in a bitter swell. Dad sucked in a deep breath and the ripple smoothed. If only the storm inside of him was as easy to quell.

Busy. Angry. Sad. And it was all my fault.

It takes a lot of power to create a god, even a baby one. At some point during her pregnancy, mom realized she didn't have enough to bring me into the world and survive. I'll never know why she didn't just ask my father to share more power with her. Maybe she was afraid he'd say no and I'd never be born. Giving birth to me killed her.

Dad took a deep breath and rested a hand on the arm of his throne. "These lessons matter. If you don't learn this . . ." He raked his fingers through his short, spiky hair, sending little air bubbles into the water around him. "You cannot afford obscurity."

That was a lesson hard learned. My dad always said that my mother was the most beautiful goddess in the four realms. Unfortunately she was shy. Like, so shy that if I'd asked three different people who the queen of the ocean realm was, I'd get three different answers since pretty much no one was sure of her name. Not a good thing since gods live off worship. She'd survived for as long as she had because my dad shared *just* enough power to keep her alive. Until I came along and sucked it all away.

"As the heir to this realm, you have responsibilities . . . "

He kept talking but I stopped hearing him. Literally. The room knew I needed a minute, even if he didn't so audio went out. My entire life could be reduced down to responsibilities. She'd wanted a baby, he hadn't. I shouldn't know that, but because of the way she died, I know a lot of things I shouldn't. Not like created gods, they know everything and can use all their powers right away. Born gods come into the world without knowing anything and have to grow into their powers. I lived somewhere in-between. The last of her powers had awakened some of mine and given me a lot of knowledge I shouldn't have with gaps the size of oceans.

Audio came back full force. " . . . residents of the realm will rely on you and *your* powers to survive. That should matter enough to be on *time!*"

"I know." I hated how weak my voice sounded. When Mom faded away, I was left with a debt I would never be able to pay back, a burden I never asked for, and a dad who never wanted me in the first place. But however he felt about *me*, my dad loved *her*. And since I was all that was left of her, Dad was determined that I'd avoid her fate.

"If I can take time off from running a realm to teach you, you can damn well make time to learn."

"I know. I just lost track of time."

"Lost track of time? *Lost track of time!*" He was really getting warmed up now. "Of all the irresponsible, selfish things-- it's once a *week* Triton, hardly a demanding schedule."

Dad channeled bits of power to me once a week and taught me how to use them. Then he poured scraps of his leftovers into the conch shell I always carried on me, just in case I ran into some kind of an emergency and needed a bit of divine assistance beyond my own abilities.

I used to cling to that shell as proof that he cared, even if most of the time he couldn't really meet my eyes. Having a piece of him with me was better than nothing, right? He didn't *have* to give me anything, so why would he unless I meant something to him.

But gods can't lie, even to themselves. If he really cared, he'd make time more than once a week and he wouldn't waste it yelling at me. I'd take his stupid lessons because I saw the sense in them. Whenever I was old enough to come into my powers on my own, I was going to make such a big splash that no one would ever forget my name. Then he'd know I didn't need him anymore. One less responsibility for Dad, one less burden for me.

Dad sucked in a breath so he could keep yelling. "Do you even *realize—*"

Pulse.

Somewhere far away, three drops of golden blood dripped into the ocean. Dad broke off with a curse as power rippled through the realm. "I have to go."

"What *is* that?" I demanded, hair standing on end.

"Demeter...she's in trouble, I have to *go!*" Without another word, Dad vanished.

Demeter, as in the goddess in charge of the human realm Demeter? No chance of me staying here then! Dad gave me teleportation authorization as soon as I was big enough to swim. The Circle may be safe from humans, but danger still lurked around every corner and he wanted me to be able to escape in the blink of an eye. But with that borrowed power came limitations. He'd made me promise not to teleport out of The Circle without him until I came of age. Since gods can't lie, that meant I literally could not break my word. But teleporting now wouldn't be breaking my word. After all, I was going with him. He just didn't know I was tagging along.

Luck was with me. I ported in just behind an outcropping of large rocks jutting from the ocean.

"Gah!" I threw my hands over my eyes and blinked fast in a desperate attempt to adjust to the sunlight. The surface was always so *bright*. I didn't understand how humans could possibly prefer that harsh white-hot light over the soft filtered-blue of the ocean.

When my eyes stopped watering, I squinted to see two figures fighting on top of a patch of land so small it could only be a sand bar. A man in dark clothing was beating the living daylights out of a girl.

No.

Not the girl.

Rubbing my eyes, I leaned closer and realized that he wasn't actually touching *her*. His hits glanced off the air around her like some kind of invisible barrier knocked them back.

A shield, I realized. Which meant this girl was a goddess. A young one, assuming she wasn't wearing a glamour.

The man in black didn't seem too worried about the shield protecting the girl. He just kept on hitting her. How long could she keep it up?

Where was Dad? I glanced around but all I saw was the endless blue of the sky meeting the sea. There was no one else who could help. That tiny bit of sandbar and the two deities struggling on it were the only other bit of color for miles. It was up to me to save her.

My fin split into legs as I grabbed my conch shell and lifted my head up high. Scenes from a million movies and shows played out on the tiny screen of my cell phone flashed through my mind. I suppressed a grin. Who was about to rescue a damsel in distress and get his first kiss? This guy.

I'd just gathered enough energy to port and surprise the crap out of the man in black when the girl darted out from behind her shield to grab his arm. I knew, I just knew she was about to do something epic.

"What is going on here?" Dad's voice, laced with enough power to twist my stomach in knots, echoed off the shore.

I darted behind the outcropping of rocks, my head whipping back and forth to find him. Had he seen me? Oh man, I was gonna be in so much trouble!

Several yards to my left, Dad strode through the waves to the shore. He must have shielded himself to take stock of the situation before interfering. Had he seen me?

Before Dad reached the sand, the man in black teleported away.

Dad stepped closer to the girl and asked her something in a low murmur that carried so much worry in it that my mouth dropped open. He'd . . . never sounded like that before. Ever.

She didn't seem to care.

"I had him!" The girl spun on him, green eyes glittering with rage. "You ruined everything!"

Holy crap, he was going to kill her for talking to him that way! I gripped my conch shell and started forward, one hand still clinging to the rock because I didn't exactly want to out myself to Dad, but it sure felt like I needed to do something.

" . . . didn't get a good look at the other guy..." Dad's voice sounded dry but otherwise he didn't seem like he was about to pop a blood vessel.

Wh . . . why was he okay with her talking to him like that? I'd shown up five minutes late to god lessons, but she could outright yell at him? What was this?

The girl cradled her wrist to her chest and drew in a sharp breath like she was about to yell some more, but before she could get the words out, she coughed. The wet hacking sound was so terrible that even I could tell it meant something really, really bad.

Dad swore and stepped onto the beach.

"Stay back!" she yelled.

" . . . helping you."

" . . . don't want to owe you . . ."

The wind picked up, snatching their words away from me and stirring the water into mini-waves that stung as they slapped against my skin. I shivered; it was cold on the surface world. Who knew?

Dad's shoulders stiffened, but instead of getting mad, he tried to reason with her.

" . . . not thinking clearly." He stepped toward her, arm outstretched.

Now her voice rang out loud and clear. "Don't touch me!"

"Persephone—"

Not Demeter then.

"Don't come one step closer! This might not be much land, but it's still earth, and you are *not* welcome here." She stamped her foot and the ground trembled. "This is my realm. Get out!"

When Dad stepped closer, the ground rose up beneath him, shoving him back into the water.

"Get *back*!" Her voice sounded raw from screaming.

Whoa. She was strong. *Really* strong. But she was also hurting. I could see it in the way she carried herself. And there was something else. Something familiar in her stance.

Dad held one hand out and kept trying to reason with her. Part of me wondered what it was about this girl he was so invested in, but the rest of me held my breath to see if he'd be able to help her.

Dad kept his voice patient and calm, as if he was talking to a wild animal, " . . . not going to hurt you . . ."

"Stay away from me," she warned when his foot crept toward the sand.

"It isn't your realm, you know. It's your mother's," my father pointed out.

She was Demeter's daughter, I realized. And she obviously had control over the realm, so she was a realm heir like me.

"You don't get to talk about my mother. I know what you did."

Dad drew back like she'd *done* something to him and I found myself wondering what he'd done. " . . . long time ago—"

"You're scum! You're worse than scum. And I am never ever going to put her in the position of owing you *anything*. Least of all my life. Now step *back!*"

He raised his hands in surrender. "Can you teleport to Hades?"

To *Hades?* He wanted to send her to Hades? No wonder she was pissed.

Tears glittered in her eyes. "He'll just be waiting for me in Tartarus. I'll never make it."

When Dad stepped onto the beach, she stiffened, voice going hard. "If you come any closer, I'll let Hades think you did this to me."

Hades. God of the Underworld. Now *that* was a threat. But why would Hades care one way or another what happened to this girl?

Dad stepped back into the water. "If I don't help you, you are going to die."

What was he talking about? Gods can't die. But they couldn't lie either. The girl winced and seemed to shrink in on herself. Why was she in pain? What was wrong with her?

"Why not skip Tartarus?" Dad asked.

"I can't teleport between realms."

"So make an entrance."

Make an entrance? I sucked in a breath. The only people who could make entrances between realms were realm rulers. But...she wasn't much older than I was. How—

A deep rumbling filled the air. The water went choppy and the rock I hid behind vibrated so much I worried it was about to break into a million pieces. I grabbed hold of the rock as the water sloshed around me. When the rumbling stopped, the girl was gone.

AS SOON AS I PORTED home, I shifted back to fins, settled onto my clamshell bed, and pulled up the search engine on my phone.

"Does that hurt?" Rhode asked as she swam into my cave. Soothing blue light danced across the pale limestone floor.

"No." Luckily the girl's name was weird enough to stick out online. "She's really seventeen." There were too many pictures of her spanning too many years for the way she looked to be a glamour. Vain gods reliving the glory days was one thing. The awkward stage before that, not so much.

"Who?" Rhode asked, swimming above me so she could see.

"Persephone." I moved my phone to the left so Rhode could see the picture around my head.

Rhode clicked in approval. "Pretty. What was she in?"

"N-nothing." As I scanned over a news article about her an icy feeling settled in my stomach. "She's a realm-heir, like me."

"Which realm?"

"Living." I shifted, trying to get comfortable on the soft-bottomed plants that filled the shell. "This rock star guy traveled to the Underworld to save his dead wife or something and met up with her there."

Rhode tilted her head in confusion, the motion tilting her body just enough to brush against mine. She jerked back and swam up a foot, releasing a stream of bubbles as she rose. "She's a psychopomp?"

I nodded, still reading. "Orpheus told everyone about her when he got back to the living realm and he's just famous enough for people to listen."

"So she has worshipers?" Rhode's voice was tinged with worry.

I shook my head. There were people who believed in us, but not many. "Mostly everyone seems to think he got into some heavy drugs and hallucinated the whole thing." I set the phone down on a rock and exchanged a look with Rhode. "But it still counts."

Gossip, speculation, it all counts as worship, which explained why this girl was so screwed up. Child gods can't handle worship. She'd need someone to channel that power away. Since she was older than me, she was probably fine to handle the initial gossip, but then things got worse. Some tabloid reporter had seen her with Orpheus and snapped a picture right before his wife miraculously woke up from her coma. It hadn't taken long to put a name to her face. Now people knew her name, her face, where she lived, everything.

"Is she going to be okay?" The worry in Rhode's voice reflected my own, and for one gut churning moment, I allowed my thoughts to shift in a direction I never let myself think about.

When I gave her sentience, how much of her personality was hers and how much of it was mine? I pushed away the thought. Rhode was my friend, not some weird reflection of me. "She's in trouble, Rhode, but I can help her."

"How can I help?"

"See this?" I held up my shell, wondering why I was even explaining this to Rhode since she wouldn't remember. "Dad uses it to store powers I'm not old enough to handle. Demeter must not know about how to do this, but if I show her . . ."

Rhode followed my train of thought. "She'll be able to do it for Persephone."

"Exactly."

"But you can't leave this realm without your Dad."

I grinned. "Leave that to me."

OVER THE NEXT few days, I sent guppies to keep an eye on my dad. But until one of them saw him teleport away, the only thing I could do was wait.

"Does that hurt?" Rhode asked as I stepped into the storage crate.

"No." I snapped, too sick with worry to bother with manners. She wouldn't remember if I was rude anyway.

"Oh. Good. Triton . . ." Rhode hovered in the doorway for a few minutes, watching as I stacked boxes. "As fascinating as this . . . collection you've got going is, people are starting to talk."

"You've told me." I was trying to make a level surface to display my collection of random human stuff, but it was hard since the whole container was tilted. Still, it was a pretty decent distraction.

"I have?" She hesitated, looking confused. Well, as confused as a dolphin possibly could, which was looked more like delighted despite mild puzzlement. "Why do you collect all this stuff?"

"I like it." I fingered a dark Metallica t-shirt I'd found in one of the boxes. What would it be like to not hit reset every time I wanted to talk to a friend? The only other person in the entire realm I could really *talk* to was my dad. And he was always busy.

Persephone would remember me.

"Yeah, kind of figured that," Rhode snarked. "But why? I mean, you're royalty. You literally have the best of the best of everything you can get down here. What's so fascinating about their trash?"

Grunting, I lifted another box wondering if it was even worth explaining again. "It's not trash. It means something." I held up the duck, mind flashing with images from all the shows and commercials I'd seen of loving parents bathing cute little children with a bop of soap on their nose. Maybe this particular duck had never been used in one of those weird, human moments complete with sappy music playing in the background, but it was the closest I was ever going to get.

A yellow and blue guppy swam to the entrance of the storage container and flapped in an awkward circle, the extent of its instruction-following abilities.

Dad had left the realm! "Gotta go." I scrambled out of the crate, legs merging back into a tail.

"Go where?" asked Rhode, bumping against me at exactly the wrong time. She let out a surprised squeal when we popped up at the outcropping of rock, now significantly smaller thanks to the tide, I'd hidden behind when I first saw the girl.

"I'm sorry, I'm so sorry." I put a hand on her slippery head to calm her down.

Rhode thrashed around in the water, eyes wild. She wasn't cussing me out, which meant I'd let speech slip somewhere in the transition. Maybe that was for the best considering what I was about to do.

Before I showed Demeter my shell, I needed to find the girl to make sure she was okay. Because if I left the realm, I was in big trouble. So if someone else had managed to help her or if she didn't need help anymore for some other reason, I'd rather find out now.

Wind whipped against me carrying the sting of salt water as I made my way toward the sand bar. My legs divided in two so I could walk when the water got too shallow to swim. Only a tiny strip of the sand remained above sea level. Hopefully it would be enough.

Holding my breath, I ran my thumb along the sharp edge of my shell. My flesh split and a tiny drop of blood welled up along the cut.

"Persephone," I whispered, letting the blood drip toward the sand. Three drops fell from my finger then whipped by me in the breeze so fast I couldn't tell where they landed. Why was wind such a big thing up here?

I crouched low to the sand, ready to try again when I heard a soft voice behind me.

"You called?"

I spun around so fast, I almost fell face first into the sand. There she stood, all but glittering in the sunlight as her blonde hair fanned around her, gently swaying in the breeze. Brilliant green eyes stared at me in speculation under heavy lashes.

"You're okay!" I ran up to her and just in time realized giving her a hug was probably a bit too familiar considering we'd never actually met. The whole speech I'd prepared on the off chance she showed up flew out of my head leaving me stuttering in disjointed fragments. "I—I saw you the other day, and I thought—I mean, you looked—I wanted to help you. To make sure you're okay."

"Who are you?" She tilted her head studying me with a calculating look in her eye. For one moment, I wondered if I'd been wrong about her being close to my age. That gleam in her eye made her seem older, wiser, and powerful enough to set my hair on end. But then her lips melted into a warm smile and the moment of doubt passed.

Cautious clicks came from the waves and I remembered Rhode. I held a hand out behind me so she'd know I heard her.

"T—Triton."

"Now there's a name I've never heard before." A slow smile played on her lips. "You must be new."

I nodded, too tongue tied to say much else.

"Are you Poseidon's son? You look just like him."

People kept saying that, but I thought maybe they were wrong. Maybe I looked more like my mom than my dad. That would explain why he couldn't look at me, anyway.

"Am I right?" She arched an eyebrow at me.

I hesitated. Dad didn't want my existence publicized just yet. Child gods don't do so well under the pressures of worship. But…this was another god, so surely the same rules didn't apply. "Yeah."

"Do you— " she broke off, clearing her throat and glancing down at the sand. When she looked up at me again, worry flickered in her eyes chased by fear. "Do you really want to help me?" Her voice broke on the word help.

"Yeah," I breathed, unable to articulate much else.

"Why? I mean, you don't even know me."

A million lines from a million shows sprang to my mind, but I pushed them aside, determined the next words would be mine.

"We're the same." I didn't just mean that we were both gods. That day that she'd screamed at my dad from this beach, I'd heard the rage in her voice, yeah, but there was something else. She was alone. Just like me. Somehow despite belonging to an epic family of gods, we were both alone and angry and scared of what we could do. Of who we could become. "We should stick together."

A smile broke across her face and she held out her hand. "Will you come with me?"

I didn't hesitate. "Yes." But I wouldn't get very far if my dad thought I'd left the realm. "Just one second." I knelt down and touched the tip of my conch shell to the water, eyes closed so I could concentrate.

I felt, rather than saw, trace bits of power pouring out of the shell and into the sea foam. One tiny push from me was all it took to send the foam in a thousand directions. If Dad tried to find me before I was ready to come back, he'd have a heck of a time trying to trace me through powers.

"I like the way you think," Persephone gushed.

"Aw, that was nothin'. Wait till you see what else I can do." I grinned and grabbed her hand, ignoring the warning call of the dolphin as the two of us disappeared.

Acknowledgments

Thanks again to my wonderful writer's group and my fantastic editor, Deb! I couldn't have done it without you. As always, a big thanks to my family for their unending support, especially Tyler for sitting through hours of editing audiobooks. No one wants to hear their sister talk that long.

About the Author

Kaitlin Bevis spent her childhood curled up with a book and a pen. If the ending didn't agree with her, she rewrote it. Because she's always wanted to be a writer, she spent high school and college learning everything she could to achieve that goal. After graduating college with a BFA and Master's in English, Kaitlin went on to write *The Daughters of Zeus* series. www.kaitlinbevis.com

Lightning Source UK Ltd.
Milton Keynes UK
UKHW040740270223
417573UK00024B/76